I0708663

# HER BILLIONAIRE
# COWBOY'S
## *Best Friend*

# HER BILLIONAIRE COWBOY'S *Best Friend*

GALLOWAY SONS FARM
A FAIR CREEK ROMANCE, BOOK 3

## CATHY SHOUSE

Copyright © 2023

All rights reserved.

This book or part thereof may not be reproduced in any form, stored in a retrieval system, or transmitted in any form by any means-electronic, mechanical, photocopy, recording, or otherwise without prior written permission of the publisher, except as provided by United States of America copyright law.

*Her Billionaire Cowboy's Best Friend*
Cathy Shouse

Interior design and formatting by:

www.emtippettsbookdesigns.com

# Chapter 1

Bree Murphy glanced out of the picture window of Delaney's Diner, wishing the cornstalks adorning the streetlamp poles would disappear. The pumpkins on the sidewalks could go away too.

Bree's chest tightened as she waited at the counter for her balloons. Her job as director of the history museum she'd inherited got harder in the fall. The annual festival she hosted was days away. If only the cute touches would attract the crowd she desperately needed for the Murphy Museum's survival and to support her and Trey through the winter. She related to some of the farmers who were in dire need of a good harvest.

"Hang on tight," Sierra Delaney, the diner's owner, said and pressed the tail end of a ribbon into Bree's fingers. A shiny green balloon shaped like a tractor bobbed toward the ceiling at the end of the string.

Bree plastered on a smile for her schoolmate, not that they knew one another well. "This balloon is perfect. It's unbelievable that Trey's turning five."

With a shrug, Sierra started to fill another balloon, but her grin told Bree she was pleased with the compliment. "These have been a hit with my youngest customers." Or maybe Sierra always smiled, since the last time their paths had crossed had been when Sierra married Wyatt Galloway in a double wedding, becoming an instant family when she'd adopted his toddler son, Max.

Bree held in a sigh. Some people's families came together more easily than others.

"Other kids adore dinosaurs, but my Trey loves all things farming."

"Really? Max likes living on the farm, but he's used to it. He's currently obsessed with construction equipment, since his daddy's doing some building at the family farm."

Bree pushed her words out past the lump in her throat. "Makes total sense." Her son wouldn't be introduced to farming or construction equipment by his father.

Two more balloons waited to be filled. Too bad Bree's spirits were as deflated as the limp latex laying on the counter. She was pretty sure it'd take more than a shot of chemical gas to lift her up. Trey's dad would have to appear out of thin air.

Bree gathered up the inflated balloons, paid for them, and started toward the door. God had a plan, and she needed to keep focused on her work, which was to save her family's museum. It held a history that was significant to others too. At this point, it was also Trey's legacy, a record of the only family he had known.

She wouldn't dwell on her troubles today when she still needed volunteers to help with the festival and time was short. She was preserving more than her family's history, since it was intertwined with the town's and included Dale Murphy's artifacts. A pang of regret came over her that the cowgirl movie star who was Dad's cousin had died young and she'd never gotten to meet her.

On her way through the dining area, she almost stumbled over a table, and the older man sitting closest to her reached out. She caught herself without his help. "Hey, I love balloons. Thanks for thinking of me," he teased, pretending to take the balloons as a gift.

"Nice try, but these are for my little man, Trey." Bree smoothed her hair with one hand and tightened her grip on the balloons, then addressed the other men at the table. "Hey, there's a rumor that you all raised funds and put in the playground equipment at the park. It's one of Trey's favorite places now."

The man's expression softened. He probably had grandkids. Grandparents were also missing from Trey's life. Sheesh, what was with her today? She'd channeled Bree, the Debbie Doom version, apparently.

The man offered his hand to shake. "I'm Ted Mitchell. So happy to hear your son's enjoying our efforts, Miss Murphy."

What? He knew her name? Strangers knowing things about her wasn't her favorite thing about Fair Creek. The bell over the diner's door jingled and she shook off the thoughts.

She gave them a bright smile and rubbed her hand on the shoulder closest to the balloon until the muscle loosened. "You can call me Bree. All my friends do."

Ted didn't skip a beat. "Bree, can we help you with anything?" There were smiles all around.

She hesitated, wondering if they were giving lip service or were serious. But the Lord had laid on her heart to count her blessings, and the townspeople had been so kind since she and Trey had come back to save the museum. Just moments ago, these men had struck up a conversation, trying to ease her load.

"Well, since you asked–" Bree held out her free hand and ticked out a finger each time she named something. "Judges for the parade to give out awards for the floats. Judges for the Dale Murphy look-a-like contests, both children and adults. Helpers for the kiddie tractor pull."

Ted clanked his spoon on his mug as he removed it and took a sip before answering. "That's good, for starters. We're in the car club that's putting on the Dale Murphy Cruise-In. That shouldn't interfere—only one conflict or two that I can see."

Her shoulders relaxed. The events she'd listed had been held at the same time for decades, so everybody knew when they happened. "That'll be a big help. I've got others still on my list to ask."

"Here's your usual!" Sierra approached the table with plates of breakfast food in hand and platters arranged halfway up one arm.

"We'll need the extra energy," Ted said with a chuckle, patting his stomach. "The festival's coming up and we've got jobs to do." The men in his posse nodded vigorously.

Bree smiled, stepped away from the table, and headed toward the door. "Thanks so much. I'll get you the details later."

She maneuvered with the balloons through the door and out onto the sidewalk. Freed into the outside world, the balloons bounced above the doorway, toward the blue-gray sky with a few off-white clouds. Bree tightened her grip, her nails digging into her palm. She inhaled the earthy scent in the air mixed with cut grass from somebody's newly mowed lawn. The wheat and soybean fields bordered Fair Creek, Indiana so closely it was almost like living on a farm.

Yeah, right. She couldn't kid herself that she and Trey were farmers.

She might have actually missed all of this when she'd been away for several years—maybe a little. Her feelings about Fair Creek were sometimes the definition of a love-hate relationship.

Near the curb, she reached into her purse that dangled from her shoulder and located her car keys.

"Bree."

She froze. That voice. It couldn't be.

Only one person had ever drawled her name like that, stretched out like a verbal caress. Her fingers loosened and the balloons started to release. She regained her grip and snuck a sideways peek at the man. Wavy brown hair along his shirt collar showed under his cowboy hat, and in profile, his distinctive jawline was unmistakable.

Her best friend from high school leaned in and loosely slipped a muscled arm around her shoulder. "It's good to see you, darling." A whiff of an expensive scent mixed with something woodsy filled her senses. Time seemed to move in slow motion, but only a few seconds could have passed. Seeing the balloons rising above her alerted her she'd lost her grip.

The familiar voice repeated her name, sharper than before. More than a head taller, he just managed to grab the strings Sierra had anchored for her into a bundle. After pulling them down to her level, he returned it. Their fingers brushed, and the warmth caused her to pull away as if she'd been burned. What was wrong with her? They'd only ever been best friends.

Well, if she didn't count that one night. "Gage Galloway. Uh, I never figured you for some kind of balloon whisperer." Her voice sounded a bit high, but maybe he wouldn't notice. Hopefully, he couldn't detect the mental meltdown happening in her brain either.

They faced one another and he laughed, the same hearty way she'd appreciated throughout their friendship. "I'm more of a shouter, but you can call me whatever you want, darling. Just as long as you call me."

They'd always kidded around. At that line spoken in his deep bass voice, and some drawl he'd picked up who-knew-where, Bree's heart hammered in her chest. "You never used the word 'darling' in the past. And phone lines work both ways, you know." That came out a little harsher than she'd intended. All the times she'd called and tried to reach him bubbled up in her mind.

Gage stepped over and leaned against the diner's exterior, then gazed into her eyes more intently. "Go figure. Putting on Dad's old cowboy hat when I arrived changed me. I can't argue with you about phones working both ways, except when they don't."

She couldn't help rolling her eyes. "They told me communication with you was 'severely compromised.'" Her fingers made air quotes around the words. "I don't give up easily, but they'd put me in an endless loop of transferred calls. If I reached a live person, and a lot of the times the phone disconnected before I did, they'd explain that you were unreachable."

A crease appeared on his forehead and he quirked an eyebrow. "I can't believe it was *that* hard to get through."

"I started the process time and time again with the same result. Then I'd see you on the nightly news covering a war zone. It was maddening and downright scary."

She couldn't believe he was here. It didn't seem real.

*Maybe this was God's plan.*

When Bree had thought of this moment, she'd never pictured it outside of Delaney's. Anybody in town might walk by, which wasn't going to be a huge number. But still. "You've never let anything stand in your way, Gage. Oh, and I don't remember you as being loud. More like determined." Her heart raced, and her breathing was ragged.

That cowboy hat tilted on his head enhanced the chocolate shade of his eyes that could compete with the cowboys in the movies Granny had gotten her hooked on. "Some things don't change, darling. You were always one of the smoothest talkers in these parts."

There was that drawl again, and he was surely pulling her leg. "That's saying something, coming from you, an award-winning international journalist."

He removed his hat. "Trust me, the TV station promo staff were full of more hot air than your balloons there." With his thick, dark hair, slightly crooked nose from getting broken in school, he still took the prize for the best-looking man she'd ever seen.

"Nice try at being modest." She grinned. "You have a lot to be proud of, and I'm happy for you."

Gage stared as if he were waiting for her to say more. Bree inhaled. The years hadn't changed him much, except for a few additional laugh lines around his eyes that made him more handsome. Their different personalities had kept them in the friend zone. He'd probably been too busy to think about her. She'd been reminded of him every day since the test stick showed pink.

"Welcome home, Gage. Somebody said you were coming, but I didn't have details."

"Keeping the lawyers happy and checking in on the family. The London bureau was more of a mess than they let on to get wrapped up."

Her throat was sandpaper. "Planning ahead wasn't your thing either. Must be an impromptu visit. Never knew where you'd be, and when you covered the military overseas, that was something else."

*Stop babbling*, she thought. *Don't let him suspect somebody knows his history better than he does.* But she couldn't resist following along with where he'd been.

He rubbed the back of his neck like he used to when he was uncertain. Maybe he had thought about her? "Seeing the world was important to me since I was a little kid, and that's what I did."

She fluffed her bangs that her internal heat had glued to her forehead. No meltdown here. Nothing to see at all. "You talked about travel when we met in second grade. We bonded over cookies. It took years to figure out we were opposites. I used to think that all sounded so exciting and envied you."

"It's unbelievable what I've seen and done." His voice trailed off. "Well, most of it, anyway. Dodging the enemy, that I wouldn't recommend."

She should have told him that last time they'd seen one another. Nine months ago, they had both gone solo to the Galloway family's double Christmas weddings at the farm. But Bree had kept it really light then. Line dancing hadn't left much room for conversation, especially not on life-altering subjects. He'd only stayed a couple of hours after the ceremony, then rushed off to his all-important work.

"I was involved in putting down roots here, where I needed to be. I mean, real everyday life can be pretty compelling too. We never really agreed on that, did we?"

"Mommy! Mommy, can I have a balloon?" Trey came running, with his babysitter lagging behind him. Bree had been so involved in conversation she didn't notice the sitter had parked at the curb.

Trey calling to her melted Bree's heart, as seeing her boy always did. No mother whose baby was as sick as Trey had been at birth would take him for granted. Bree shot up a prayer of thanks, for the millionth time.

But the cowboy standing right behind her was about to get the shock of his life. Now what? There was nothing she could do to cushion the news.

# Chapter 2

Bree had a child?

Gage Galloway must have gotten heatstroke from the beating sun. That was all he could figure. He'd strewn together comp and vacation time to meet his short-term commitment to the family farm. After barely climbing off his private jet, he'd stumbled into Bree Murphy in front of Delaney's. Her blonde hair and blues eyes were as striking as ever. The years had added some pounds and only made her shapely figure more breathtaking.

Bent down to a child's level, Bree spoke. "Mommy bought these balloons for you. Happy birthday, Trey!" She hugged the little boy.

When they'd seen one another again in December, she wasn't married. That he knew for sure because she wasn't wearing a ring. He'd noticed everything about her that evening.

"I'm five!" He held up the fingers of one hand, so proud he'd show a complete stranger. The kid really was cute.

"Yes, that's the number of balloons I have here!"

Gage swallowed the lump in his throat. They seemed crazy about each other. All that travel hadn't given him any time for a relationship, let alone a family. He hadn't wanted one either. So why did he feel such a pain deep down in his gut?

He needed to focus here.

Wait. The boy had dark hair, just like his nieces and nephews. The Galloway family had a passel of little kids he'd caught up with at Christmas. They strongly resembled this one.

His mouth went dry as he did mental math. Seemed like longer than five years since he and Bree had gotten carried away saying goodbye. Really, he blamed himself for holding a secret crush on his best friend.

He'd been urgently assigned to cover the war overseas and the signal had been bad. The assignment had stretched on, and they'd been out of touch for so long. With no word from her, he'd obviously gotten the answer that she didn't feel the way he had.

Mother and child were wrapped up in each other, talking about chocolate and ice cream. The boy's eyes went to the bright-colored latex above his head. "Can I hold 'em?"

"Not today. They almost blew away a minute ago." She stood and took a step back toward Gage. "Thankfully, my old friend here helped me."

The woman who brought the child had a phone alarm that

sounded off, and she spoke to Bree. "So sorry to interrupt. But when you seemed to be running late, I thought I might get lucky and meet you here and grab the balloons, since the Fair Creek preschool is right down the street. I'll deliver them for you."

Bree seemed tongue-tied about as much as he was. She didn't go further into introducing him, just handed the balloons over to the woman and hugged her child. "I'll see you after work and we'll have a real celebration. Now, don't get into too much cake before we're together at your party, okay?"

The boy, who looked more and more like him—the nose and forehead too—nodded solemnly. "Bye, Mommy." Trey went half-skipping, half-running to the car. The balloons swirled behind the woman up into the bright blue sky. If only Gage could be so carefree.

Gage swallowed as his heart pounded in his ears. The resemblance was striking. Could there be an explanation? He had three brothers. All were settled down though.

The child had to be his.

*Don't you dare faint.* The thought ran through Bree's mind while standing in front of Delaney's. But she'd never be so lucky. She'd have to face Gage. *Lord, help.* She couldn't escape his frown and the way his eyes sparked with fire. Trey's eyes were that same dark-chocolate brown that she loved.

"Why didn't you tell me?" The anguish in Gage's tone about

killed her. He was either choking back emotion or lashing out in anger. She wasn't sure which.

"I planned to tell you and tried to reach you from the beginning. I couldn't ever get anyone to connect me with you."

"You didn't try hard enough." The words came through clenched teeth.

"Is everything all right?" Ted Mitchell stepped out onto the sidewalk after leaving the diner, and his friends trailed along behind.

Gage's frown lessened and he spoke in an even tone. "We're just having a discussion. Good to see you, Ted."

The men walked on but having them there had taken some of the heat out of both of them.

Bree headed two store fronts down to the empty bench in front of Vintage Finds antique store, which was closed during the week. When Gage followed, the tension in her chest subsided a little. "Gage, our baby was born premature and with a heart defect. He consumed my thoughts and energy 24/7." In those long days and even longer nights, she'd thought about Gage and prayed for Trey's daddy to come back home safe.

"That must have been terrifying. But he looks so healthy and energetic."

She perched on one edge of the bench. "He had open heart surgery before he was one. They tell me he'll be fine, but he gets checked regularly."

Gage slumped down on the opposite edge of the bench. "I

can't believe you couldn't reach me."

"I called when I could. At one point, a woman promised to give you the message. I waited and waited. Still heard nothing."

He seemed at a loss, so she plunged on. "I wanted to tell you at the Christmas weddings, but everybody said you were flying in and out to some important thing. Who knew we'd end up dancing together all night?" Her voice shook and she took deep breaths for calmness.

He stretched his legs out in front of him, shoving his hands into his pockets and then pulling them out. He'd done that in speech class out of nervousness when they were high school sophomores and quit it soon after.

He was the injured one here. Mouth bone dry, she attempted to swallow. "I'm sorry. I know that's not enough. But I mean it. And I hope you can forgive me."

"It doesn't even come close to adequate. Why didn't anyone else tell me?"

"When I found out, I moved away from Fair Creek. Took a job from a family friend with a business who needed some office help. They let me bring him in with me. It was low-key."

"Would have been simpler to be here."

"Mom came every weekend, stayed with us for long stretches too."

"Being a single mother must have been more difficult in a new place." He didn't speak with any emotion.

She felt hollow inside. But they had to get through this to get to the other side, wherever that led. "I prayed and felt it was easier if I went away. Not out of shame, because he was meant to be born. I have no doubt God has plans for him. But I left because of the circumstances, to protect us both."

Fair Creek was such a tiny town and farm community. The Galloways were the biggest farm family and were everywhere she went. They'd been best friends and had only found more feelings the night he was going away for good. There was no way to explain all of that to people when she couldn't explain it to herself.

He took off his cowboy hat and replaced it. "I respect the decisions you've made in taking care of him, Bree. I wasn't here. You've put his needs first and it shows."

He wasn't one to express emotions, except in his writings. In the sleepless nights in the aftermath of their indiscretion, she concluded a lack of openness about feelings had to be why two normally level-headed friends had ended up in such a situation.

Someone needed to fill in the gap here. "My living in the city probably saved his life." Gage's forehead creased and his hands went back into his pockets. "We lived within a mile of the most prestigious children's hospital in the Midwest."

Gage got up and paced up and down the sidewalk, which was thankfully empty. "I'm so glad you both came through well. I want to be involved with him like I should have been all along. To be his dad. I don't know how to make up for lost ground and the times I wasn't there. Of course, I'll pay all the back child support and everything going forward. What do you need?"

Bree stood up to face him. Tears pricked at the back of her

eyes. Don't you dare cry, she thought to herself.

"It's been a long five years." She breathed in and focused on what needed to be said. "I love him to pieces, and we've struggled, especially after Mom died. I'm not asking you for anything. What he needs is a dad. He needs you, not your money."

Gage rested a hand lightly on her arm. "He'll have both. I'm here for him…and for you… I couldn't figure out why I was led to come back here."

His hand dropped away and he resumed pacing, while she slumped onto the bench, missing his closeness.

"After Dad died, his will required me to participate in the farm somehow. But everything that's happened has brought me back here, to temporarily manage Galloway Sons Farm while Caleb takes a break. Guess only God knew the real reason."

She sniffed. "We'll figure it all out. This is going to be his best birthday ever, and he doesn't even know it."

"I want to be at the party. I've missed him being born and four birthdays already."

Was she ready for Gage Galloway to see where she lived at her family's museum? The man had loads of money and wouldn't be impressed with her living arrangements. Would she lose Trey over this? She wanted to do what was right by Trey, and he needed to know his father. Having a fancy party like some of the other kids did was out of the question. She was barely keeping afloat. There weren't any extras.

"Of course, you will be."

The corners of his mouth twitched up for the first time and

her heart broke a little. "That would mean a lot. He's my son, after all."

She nodded. "You'll be in his life from here on out." What could she do in a couple of hours to make things better? She stood to go. Working at the museum wasn't about the pay, which wasn't good. Her family's heart and soul had gone into the museum, and by preserving it for herself and Trey, she hoped to help the town too. And there were the medical bills. She'd been up late last night putting the finishing touches on the homemade cake shaped like a tractor, since hiring a baker wasn't in her budget.

"I've tried to forgive myself for that last night we were together. Anger at you for keeping him from me doesn't seem right. Everybody makes mistakes."

"It wasn't a mistake. Start with that. Trey was an unexpected blessing." She smiled that this conversation was almost behind her. "Look, I've really got to get back. I live above the museum. Come at 6:00 p.m. and see a batch of five-year-olds transcend on my place."

"That gives me time to get a gift. What does Trey like? I want to know all about him. I'll start with a present, if you'll help me out."

What a question. There were no easy answers. "He's all boy, Gage. You're gonna love him. Everybody does." Her phone beeped. "I've got to get back to the museum."

"I don't see how I can let you go like this."

"Well, you'll have to. Wasn't that hard the last time. *You* could have called *me*."

"So you *are* mad." He used to sound grumpy and now he growled. "Good to know. I *was* busy at work and off the grid. But I also was devastated I'd damaged our friendship, the best relationship I'd ever had." He raked his fingers through his hair. "I should have known something was up. All you wanted to do was dance at the weddings, not talk and catch up. We used to talk so much."

"I wasn't trying to deceive you. I really wasn't. But after that night when we said goodbye, I felt we needed to find our way back to friends. Dancing my cares away did me a world of good."

"This is so hard to believe." His growl was back. She couldn't blame him. How would they ever get past this and be able to co-parent? The Gage she'd known wouldn't take her baby, but she didn't know him anymore, not really.

"Well, you were busy telling me your next assignments and everything you had planned. You sort of validated what I'd always thought. Knowing you had an unexpected child in your life, with your best friend, no less? I'm not going to say it would have ruined your life, but it would have really altered it. You'd always made it clear you didn't want kids. I felt irresponsible for not, being prepared."

"Look, I was there. Neither of us anticipated—"

This subject needed tabled. "Hey, I walked over here and needed to get out. But I gotta run." She started walking toward the museum.

"I made you late. Let me at least drive you two blocks?"

She wanted to be alone, but at least they weren't totally at odds. "That'll save me a little time. Thanks."

She hadn't kept Trey from him to hurt him. If anything, her time apart from Gage had taught her the reason they'd been friends and nothing more. She liked everything in order, and he ran on the wild side. Having kids had always been part of her plan and never anywhere on his radar. She devoted herself to Trey and her family's memories in the museum. Gage didn't even stay in touch with his family.

He headed toward a vehicle, and she followed. "So, what's going on with the museum?"

She waited for him to open the passenger door for her. "It's a challenging time. I think we'll pull through." She offered up a prayer that her words would be true.

A minute later, they were started down the street toward the museum.

"History was always your passion, wasn't it? I always thought you'd figure out a way to work in it."

"After we said our goodbyes, I was heading to school to study history, remember?"

"My own future had me all wrapped up in traveling and getting to cover world events. That was all-consuming, and I didn't think of anybody else." He shook his head and looked across the cab at her. "I was pretty bad, wasn't I?"

He turned his gaze to the road and pulled out from the town's one stoplight. Bree was glad he couldn't see the confirmation in her eyes. "I was thrilled for you and the opportunities you had ahead. Even though we didn't intend to get as close as we did in our goodbye, I've loved thinking of you out there living your dream."

"You've always been such a supportive person. It makes me feel good that you weren't thinking bad things about me. Not too terrible at least?"

"Well, it's true. Except for maybe those times when reality set in that I was shouldering being a single mom with a really sick baby."

"Darling, if I'd been in your shoes, I'd have used that picture of us in our caps and gowns as a dart board."

# Chapter 3

Gage knocked on the door of the Victorian house that held the Fair Creek Museum, with a wrapped gift in his hand. Last time he'd been here, the $4^{th}$ grade class walked over from the school as part of their Indiana history lesson.

Children's voices wafted out to him on the porch. One of them was likely his son. His heartbeat thrummed in his chest. Could this really be happening? A few seconds later, the door opened. Bree smiled, and when she realized it was him, her face flushed slightly. "I wasn't sure if you'd show, honestly." She reached for the gift, and he released his grip that had been tighter than necessary.

Tight-lipped, he tried to match her cheery tone. "Wouldn't have missed it for the world." As he said the words, he knew they were true. "Oh, and don't look too closely at the wrapping." A few hours to sort things through, and that drive in the country had done him good. This would be fun, if he played it right.

She nodded. "No judgment here. For the record, I'm not surprised to see you. Even when you had your head in the clouds, I could always rely on you." She turned toward the inside of the room. "Step this way. Watch where you're going. Six boys with miniature toy cars can spread them everywhere."

"Can't be anything like watching for cow patches around the farm."

"Eww. You have a point. A misstep wouldn't have nearly the consequences either."

His gaze automatically searched for Trey. His son. He needed to get comfortable with the idea. There he was. His dark features separated him from the others.

Bree watched him, and he wondered if she could read his thoughts. They'd spent so much time together as kids. But they were very different. "We live upstairs," she said. "But this room down here is the biggest. Since all the artifacts are behind glass, they can't damage anything."

He stood there frozen, trying not to stare at Trey, but he couldn't look away. She tapped his shoulder. "Follow me to those balloons marking the gift table. Thanks again for rescuing those for me."

That seemed like forever ago, before he knew about Trey. Would his whole life be like that, BT and AT? Before Trey and After Trey? *Would that be so bad?*

She deposited his gift on the table with the others. His was the largest gift and it gave him satisfaction. "We've got punch over here. Trey insisted on a red theme so it's fruit punch we used to drink out of cans. It's the worst color on the carpet so hopefully nobody spills it."

She was rattling on, and he didn't know how to help her.

His mouth did seem unnaturally dry. "Sounds delicious."

Once he had punch in his hand in a paper cup with a red pickup truck parked next to an old red barn on it, he settled in. It wasn't an adult drink but that didn't matter.

Activity swirled around him. They played pin the tail on the cow. The cow was cleaner than any Gage had ever seen, with a flower between its teeth. But he would have plenty of time to teach his son about real cows, and the idea pleased him more than he expected.

They trooped outside and took turns bashing at a pinata shaped like a tractor hanging from a low tree limb in the little front yard. Most of them missed. Bree ended up giving it a sharp bash. When all the candy burst out onto the grass, the kids fell onto it like bees to honey.

"Letting him have a sugar high this once." She shrugged. "It never hurt us as kids. But I'm usually pretty careful with his nutrition."

Strange, talking about food habits of five-year-olds. This was new. "So it'll be my job to spoil his dinner then, darling?"

She studied him. "That's up for negotiation." She went to a large wooden cabinet with a high shelf and came back and handed him a wand to light the candles.

She seemed so much more comfortable with this than him. But she'd had years of practice. For his demanding job, he'd been told what to do and when. He'd looked forward to some freedom running his own life at Galloway Sons Farm, covering for Caleb. Now he was going to be in charge of somebody else? At least, part of the time.

Next thing he knew, six little voices, off-key and nearly screaming, sang "Happy Birthday." A sensation like his heart softening overtook him. Oh, to be so young and carefree. He joined in and couldn't remember when he'd had so much fun.

With Bree's instructions, Trey stopped, closed his eyes, and made a wish, then blew out his candles. Maybe one day, Gage would know what his son dreamed of.

Getting everyone a piece of cake with a scoop of ice cream on a paper plate looked like herding cats, as Mom used to say. How Mom would have loved this sight. Both of his parents gone now, he might have done something differently if he'd known they'd both be passed before he came back.

"Time to unwrap gifts!" She sounded a lot like a gameshow host. "Now, sit on the floor around the table so you can see the birthday boy!"

He'd spent more than an hour and gone to two stores to find exactly what he wanted for Trey, what he thought he might like best. A quick prayer to show him the right thing might have been involved. The riding vehicles that were self-powered had caught his eye, but it might be too extravagant coming from someone the child had never met, and he had seen some friends' children get spoiled young and not turn out to be responsible teenagers. Gage had spent a lifetime it felt like, always fighting to be recognized for himself and not his reputation or money, and he wanted to start off his relationship with his son on the right foot. He hoped to be close without being clouded by things. A divorced dad he knew became the weekend gift-giver and Gage wanted so much more.

Trey got hold of a corner and ripped off the paper. A realistic, toy-sized red tractor and matching wagon, encased in cardboard, appeared.

The boy's mouth dropped open. "Wow! Wow!" He stood and nearly danced. "Look, Mommy! Get it out."

Bree asked a woman Gage knew was another mom, from her T-shirt that said so, if she could bring her something to open the box.

"Trey, I'll get it out for you, but first, thank the person who gave this to you." She nodded in Gage's direction where he stood by himself, the only guy in the room, which now registered.

"Thank you!" the boy called. He braced himself for questions, but it didn't seem to register with the child that a stranger had given such a special gift.

"You're welcome!" Gage nearly choked on the words. All that he'd missed in his kid's life, and he showed such gratitude for a toy. It was wrong that he hadn't known his child existed for all this time. *Why, God?*

He shook off the thoughts and, from across the room, Bree's eyes were searching him out until they made contact with Gage's.

The intensity of her gaze conveyed there was more to do, but she dipped her head in the direction of his gift. He relaxed, knowing she approved. The tension in his shoulders lessened.

Her focus went back to her son. "Honey, you've got these other presents. Better take a look."

Not needing to be asked twice, the boy plopped down on the floor, reached for another box, and opened it with gusto, shredding the paper as he went and tossing it into the air.

Revealing the set of clay, he burst out, "I'll make horses and cows!"

Good. A smile crossed Gage's face. He could do this. Surely, he could.

A few minutes later, although it must have been at least half an hour, Trey's young guests and a couple of mothers were going home. The last of them went through the door marked exit, reminding him this really was a history museum. The silence was almost deafening, like people said, after so much racket. His moment of relief at welcoming some peace ended, and the weight of what would happen next hung like a cloud over him.

Bree took Trey's hand in hers, turned to Gage, and gave him a solid nudge, elbow to elbow as she guided them over to a cluster of chairs left over from the musical chairs game.

Bree sat down. "Trey, come here." She pulled him onto her lap. "I've got something important to tell you."

He squirmed. "Can I get my toys?" His mom released Trey, who didn't waste any time running over to the pile of toys. He pulled out the tractor and wagon from Gage, then scrambled onto Bree's lap, with both gripped in his sturdy little hands like a vice. He had to give him credit for being a well-behaved kid, from what he'd witnessed of other kids over the years.

When he was settled, Bree started whatever she was going to say. Gage's mouth went dry. The last time he'd been so enthralled by a new beginning of this magnitude had been when he was starting his career, which came in a distant second.

She kept the boy wrapped in her arms, her cheek leaned down and grazing the top of his head. "Trey, you know I read you Bible stories sometimes at bedtime. Well, your birth was part of God's plan." The boy's sparkling brown eyes widened, and he sat up as he listened, with a wrinkle on his forehead from the intensity. "Maybe you wondered why this nice man gave you this present. See, he and I have been best friends forever, and he's your daddy."

Gage swallowed the lump in his throat, wondering how anyone could have broken the news more tenderly. Trey managed to get down off Bree's lap, his new toys still in his steely grip, and marched over to Gage.

"Have you ever seen a toy combine, Daddy?" The child in front of him had his eyes and nose.

Gage lowered his elbows to his knees to be on the same level, and after a second of finding his voice, he finally got his mouth to work. "I can sure look for one, son."

The boy nodded but just stood and continued to study him, glancing over to his Stetson, and on down to his cowboy boots. Could someone feel their heart melt? He thought his just did. "Would you like to be there with me when I'm looking for a toy combine?" His boy came over and stretched his short arms around Gage's shoulders, as far as they could go, and squeezed, then scooted back over to his mom.

# Chapter 4

Bree floated around the main room of the museum, as if walking on air, studying the level of collateral damage from the party. Her baby had a daddy to protect him now. Seeing Gage taking an interest in Trey was an answer to prayer. The care he took with their son warmed her heart and showed a dimension of Gage she'd never known existed. She liked this new development.

She surveyed the room, wondering where to start the cleanup. It was getting late, and exhaustion made her want to hurry. The birthday party had gone off without a hitch, considering five-year-old parties could turn into a free-for-all. Trey had been somewhere and came home with a blue tongue and his hair all slicked back from getting hot and sweaty playing hide-and-seek.

"You sure have one sweet boy there." Gage stood by the glass case with Dale Murphy's costume from her most famous movie. "You gave him a great party." From that angle, with his broad chest and strong jawline, Gage could star in a movie.

Wait, this was her best friend, that was all, and there were valid reasons they'd stayed in the friend zone. Those dark-brown eyes waiting for her response had not been one of them.

"Thanks, on both counts." If Gage wanted a more elaborate party for Trey, he didn't let on.

"Considering the kids ate their weight in sugar, I thought they did pretty well, darling. One miniature car thrown across the room's probably less than I threw at that age."

"Some of them can get really rowdy. That's partly why I asked that boy's mom to come with him and help me serve. I've learned the hard way mothers don't want anybody else disciplining their kids."

"Wow, I've got a lot of catching up to do on the parental front. When I was a kid, my mom welcomed being informed of what I was up to when she wasn't around—good and bad."

A warmth came over her at the mention of the woman whose house she had spent so much time in growing up. "Your mom was always so nice to me. She sure raised you right, and with five kids, she makes me look like a slacker."

His brown eyes sparkled, making Bree glad she'd brought up his mom. Trey might not have parents who were married, but she and Gage had shared a rich history together. "Mom told people once the kids outnumbered the adults, they pretty much raised themselves. Thanks for letting me help get Trey ready for bed and tuck him in."

She shrugged. "Bedtimes are sacred around here, which you needed to know. Honestly? I could have burst into tears when you read the 'Now I lay me down to sleep' prayer." She cleared her throat that had choked off unexpectedly.

"I felt pretty much the same when he said a couple of the words with me."

Bree went around picking up paper plates and plasticware from the tables. "It's so great you want to be in his life, which, I mean, I thought you would. But one never knows."

"Of course. We didn't have the kind of relationship where we ever talked about kids. But, yeah." He spoke almost reverently.

Bree swallowed the lump in her throat. A silence fell between them she wasn't sure how to fill. She'd been emotional all evening, which was somewhat the norm at Trey's past parties. Birthdays had added significance when your son had a rocky start in life. Trey's tiny body lying in that NICU bassinet, wearing a scrap of a diaper, tubes sticking out everywhere, flitted through her mind. She didn't take anything for granted when it came to Trey.

She moved toward the center of the room where a fork had dropped onto the floor, leaned down, and picked it up. "So nice of you to help clean up. Don't feel you have to."

The sparkle came back into his eyes and one eyebrow quirked up. "I crashed the party, darling. Least I can do is pick up, trying to lock down future invites."

She nodded. "Let's start with the tablecloths and taking down these fold-up tables."

Gage pulled his lanky body from a resting position and headed for the closest table near Bree. "Remember when we were sophomores on prom clean-up duty, Bree? This is our do-over." After they flipped the legs in on the table, he shouldered most of the weight to lift it, then carried it on his own to the closet she directed him to.

Watching him, a bone-deep tiredness sank in. If she stopped moving, she might not be able to get started again. So, they worked in tandem, tying up the trash bag full of paper plates, plastic forks, and napkins. Every kid must have used multiple ones, based on the size of the bag. Of course, there were the adults too.

Gage held up the lumpy black plastic sack like Santa might. "Where does this go?"

"The garbage can outside the back door, but you don't…" Before she could finish, he had pushed open the screen door and disappeared, and the thump of the bag landing in the bin reached her.

What would it be like to have help like this all the time? If anyone had asked, she would have said she was doing just fine on her own. Now she stood in a heap of gratitude to have help getting the trash out.

"That's a nice patio. I'd forgotten about it."

"I needed a place for Trey to run the endless toys he likes without getting the little wheels stuck in the grass."

"Seems like the perfect answer."

She grabbed the cloth and took Mom's glass cake plate from

the dish drainer, her one piece of elegance at a children's party. "Being a mother is like solving a puzzle every day called, 'What is best for this child?' For me anyway."

"I wouldn't have thought of it that way. Where does he play if he needs to burn off some energy?"

He was right, the backyard was small, and seemed smaller the more Trey grew.

A nudge from the back of her mind came to life, worry she'd been tamping down. "The park's right down the street with all the running area any kid would need." He was more than an old school friend visiting them. He might be judging his son's living conditions and how she was doing.

He looked at her, hesitant, like he was weighing his next comment. "On the farm, he'd have all the room to stretch out, just a step outside the door."

The plate slipped from her hands. She watched, gripped by its downward trajectory that seemed in slow motion headed toward the floor.

Gage's big, strong hand clamped around the plate just in time. "Got it."

Bree choked out a response. "Thank you. Losing that plate would have broken my heart. It was Mom's."

He smiled. "Well then it's good I saved it."

She nodded, a bit shaken. It was only a treasured plate. What if he wanted Trey? She didn't even know how long Gage would stay in Fair Creek. "Would you mind stowing it there?" Not trusting herself, she pointed to a cabinet of dishes with an open spot.

There were probably children treated less carefully than that plate. And some dearly loved kids were tied to custody arrangements that had them traveling between their parents across multiple states. Her stomach churned, imagining lawyers getting involved in her and Trey's lives. She rushed to the sink to run cool water over her fingers.

"Hey, I said would you want to meet me at the park with Trey after you're done working tomorrow?"

Bree inhaled, shut off the water, and wiped her hands on a towel. "Sorry. My mind was somewhere else."

His dark-brown eyes sparkled, and her stomach fluttered, only for a different reason. Why had they never dated? There had been conversations, actually, on keeping their friendship above all else. Getting romantically involved wasn't worth the risk. "Bree Skye Murphy. Remember I'd call you Skye because you always had your head in the clouds?"

Bree faked a smack on Gage's arm. Hitting all muscle startled her and she pulled away. She hadn't thought about him playing up her middle name in a long while. "We had fun, didn't we? The park sounds great. So many happy memories we've had there. I'll bring a picnic."

Each grabbed pairs of chairs and stored them into the closet, where they'd be ready for the next museum event or family gathering.

Minutes later, he picked up his cowboy hat, spun it on one finger, and stood at the museum's front door ready to leave.

Bree's anticipation of this moment hung in the air. It was almost like a date and time for the kiss. Except it wasn't. It was nothing like that at all. He held the key to her future in his big, strong hands.

He cleared his throat. "Look, I'm easing into this co-parenting thing. That's my intention anyway. I don't like that you kept Trey a secret. But I'm a reasonable guy, and your reasons were valid."

She let out an exhale and her shoulders relaxed. "If I could have made things different, I would have."

He put his hat back on his head. "Dancing at the wedding together and not saying a word, not even a hint? Now that's a bit harder."

She nodded, holding her breath. "First, it's not something you mention casually, Gage. I carried this secret for years. Believe me, I thought of every angle and who might get hurt in every case."

He nodded. "We'll have to try to see each other's perspective." His handsome face had only gotten more handsome. His eyes under his hat gleamed, and she didn't think he was angry, but wary. Would he ever trust her?

"I'm sorry I hurt you."

"We're going to take the plans we make for Trey nice and slow. Let's be the friends we've always been, okay?"

She couldn't stop herself from giving a quick hug. He returned the embrace, and they pulled apart. The feel of the scruff on his chin distracted her, but only for a second. "I'm good with taking things one step at a time, if you are," she said. "Thank you."

"That's exactly what we'll do then." He turned to leave and

grabbed the door handle. "See you tomorrow, Skye."

After she'd locked the door behind him, she hurried up the big stairway to the upper rooms, the sound of his nickname for her still echoing in her ears. It was so long since she'd heard that. Not since her lofty plans and big dreams translated into single motherhood and keeping a tiny museum afloat.

She wasn't going to lose Trey. Her mind sang at the realization.

But was she going to lose her heart in the process?

# Chapter 5

Gage was up early the next day after finding out he had a son. He hadn't slept much, and heading out to take care of the animals sounded good. The breeze on his face cleared his head. He was a father and had missed out on years of the kid's life. The biggest thing would be taking the boy into his family. Trey was a Galloway and would have all the advantages Gage could bring him.

Tending the animal's needs, handing a carrot to a horse, brushing another's mane, soothed him. By the time he finished clearing the stalls, he was ready to face Wyatt and let him know he was an uncle again.

What had God intended by him being a father? The idea hadn't even crossed his mind in years. In fact, he had taken on dangerous assignments that would be risky and had felt good about that, possibly sparing some of his colleagues with families from danger. And all this time, he'd been a dad and didn't know it? He couldn't wrap his head around the concept.

But God had known. That gave him great comfort, somehow.

He walked up to the main house, scaled the porch steps in two long strides, and went inside. A sense of the presence of his own father came over him. He hung up his coat in the closet, full of farm jackets, where all of Dad's coats remained—boots, too, for anyone who needed them. John Galloway had been so close with him as he was growing up, it had been difficult to leave him to start on his career that took him away from Fair Creek.

Once inside the kitchen, his shoulders sagged. He went room to room, finding no one in the house. It was getting close to noon and no preparations were going on for a meal. Oh, right, Delaney's Diner took a break from bringing in catering one day a week. Maybe as the interim farm manager, he should get things back on track with meals every weekday.

After going back through to the bedroom and sunroom and still finding no one, he headed for the barn in the distance. He'd snagged Dad's hat on a peg in the barn earlier, and it had served to put him back in rural mode. No one had come out and seen him when he first arrived, which was a relief. He'd then called this meeting with Wyatt and Leo. That was before he had important, life-changing news.

"Might as well take the bull by the horns," he mumbled under his breath as he walked. Great, now all those farm phrases would fly back into his head and out of his mouth, apparently.

He and his brothers hadn't really had a much of a relationship, but given his penchant for research, he had followed them all online, as much as possible, if and when he had a random internet connection. Given they were successful businesspeople, it hadn't been that difficult tracing them. When each had chosen to come back to the farm, that had made news too.

It was going to be different seeing them again, let alone working together. But if it didn't suit him, Caleb was coming back and would take his former role anyway. He, Annie, and her daughter, Chloe, had taken an extended cross-country trip with Kayla and her twins. Their only Galloway sister was continuing to put her life and her twin toddlers' lives in order after her months of rehab overcoming her drug addiction.

Gage wanted to do his part and was legally required to participate in some way by provisions in Dad's will. Settling into Galloway Sons Farm for a short time would allow him some space, physically and mentally. Their property consisted of a huge amount of acreage and buildings. They wouldn't necessarily run into one another constantly. Yet they could if they wanted to. He didn't know what he wanted, as far as that went.

That unsettled him. It was another thing he wasn't used to, not knowing what he wanted.

"Sorry we didn't meet you at the house like we planned," Wyatt called, coming out from the barn to greet Gage. "We've had an equipment breakdown and have been tinkering on that."

They walked into the barn together. "Might as well have gone to the house, for what good we did," Leo chimed in as soon as they came close to the tractor with parts laying all around on the ground. "Not getting anywhere with it. Can't find a good mechanic anymore, and it's the height of the season, which doesn't help."

Gage's heart rate kicked up a tad. Here was something he could sink his teeth into. Meetings weren't his thing, not like interviews and being involved where the action was. "Why didn't you say so. Can I have a look?"

Leo and Wyatt exchanged a conspiratorial look that pulled Gage back to their growing-up years. With five kids, there were always different factions taking sides. "You never wanted to admit it, but I have better mechanical skills than any of you."

Leo nodded. "We've always known. You were the one who made it crystal clear you weren't interested in getting your hands greasy. But, sure, give it a shot."

Reconnecting was so overrated. Or maybe he just needed some practice.

He laid his hat on the seat and got underneath and tinkered around the tractor. Troubleshooting using his instincts, combined with an internet search of the software in the tractor, he discussed his findings, and the three of them agreed on the fix.

Leo's brown eyes shone. "Guess you might make a decent farm manager after all."

"Better than you by a mile, Artist Boy." He'd meant it to be sarcastic but failed, and it came out too cutting.

Wyatt placed his large frame in between his brothers. "Now, now, don't want anybody to end up wrestling it out like we used to." He directed his next remark at Gage. "Want to go and check on some men working on the back fence with me? I'm down to one ATV though."

Gage took a step toward the stall where the horses were. "You take that. I'd rather go on a horse."

He wondered how efficient it was to go out to the farmhands. Why didn't Wyatt use the walkie-talkie? Or did he know cell phones had been invented? Gage wasn't going to question things for a while, just observe. Could be any number of reasons Wyatt wanted to see for himself.

Wyatt started to climb onto the ATV. "How long's it been since you were on a horse?"

"Can't say for sure. Riding a horse is like riding a bicycle. Once you learn, you never forget how."

"Since you didn't ride a bike, I'm wondering how this applies."

Gage ignored the remark and went to Louise's stall, with her name plate on the side, and patted her nose. "Want to go for a ride, girl?" She brought her large head up and down in greeting, like she was happy to see him. "I'll get your saddle and we'll go."

Once he was on her back, he started in a steady trot outside of the paddock, and Wyatt was long gone. Leo had left on the tractor.

When Gage made it into the open past the arena area, he gave Louise freedom, and she tore off across the field. The open meadow and the trees flew by, leaves still green for late September in Indiana. His chest relaxed, and he realized he'd been tense since Bree had told him the news. Looking over the vast acreage, a peace came over him. This was "God's country," and things would be all right. He shot up a prayer that he'd be able to forgive Bree's deception.

She had been right about him being hard to contact, no argument there. He would have wanted to come home and be an involved parent, even though that wasn't in his plans. He would have had a dilemma, since his career meant everything, and he was needed on his job during that time. Maybe, in time, he'd understand why things had gone the way they had.

After about twenty minutes out, he spotted Wyatt along a back fence row that obviously needed repair.

"That was one quick ride for a man who hasn't been on a horse in so long, huh, bro?" Wyatt's words were critical, but his raised eyebrow and the frown and intensity in his eyes indicated concern more than anger.

"Actually, I need to talk to you." Gage dismounted and walked Louise over to a lone tree on the property in this area. He tied her reins to the low-hanging limb.

Wyatt spoke to his two farmhands and walked over to Gage, and he knew he'd want to meet the men, just not now.

"What's up?"

"I just found out I'm a dad."

"You know how to cut to the chase, as they say." Wyatt exhaled with a loud whoosh of air. "You're the last person I'd expect to hear those words from. You sure?"

"One hundred percent certain. Bree Murphy's little four-year-old, Trey? Yesterday, he turned five, but anyway, he's mine."

The lines in Wyatt's forehead deepened. He took two steps over to Louise, patted the horse's rump, and pinned his gaze on Gage. "What are you going to do?"

"Try to make up for lost time. Haven't gotten that far with details. But I'm bringing him into our family. He deserves all the Galloways have to offer, as one of us. I hope no one has a problem with that."

"Of course, you're right. I mean, you've made it clear where you stand on having your own family though."

"Trey changes everything. I wouldn't say it's good timing to learn about him now. I hate what I've missed. But it could have been a whole lot worse, fretting about him when I was imbedded covering a war zone. Maybe God's hand was in it."

"Well, Galloways have had plenty of practice with creative family planning."

Wyatt's phone rang, and he held up a finger. "Let me take this. It's Caleb."

Gage motioned that he would step away to provide privacy, and Wyatt waved him off. "Smooth as silk," Wyatt said into the phone. "Gage is here, and he's already been an asset—fixed one of the tractors."

Gage's jaw relaxed, and he realized how much pressure he'd felt. Wyatt spoke again, "How're Kayla, Drew, and Ella getting along?"

After a minute more, Wyatt disconnected the call. "Caleb said Kayla's bonding with her twins great now that he isn't guardian. Annie's pregnancy's going fine too. He begged to come back to work to get some rest. They're wearing him out."

Gage laughed. "I'm gonna need a cheat sheet to keep all the names in this family straight, dude."

Wyatt looked out over the horizon toward his workers and chuckled. "We've grown pretty fast, but you'll get on to the kids' names real quick. They've got their own personalities."

He was surprised to feel as if he might have let them down. "Kayla might have needed some support after getting out of rehab. I'm sorry I wasn't here."

"Caleb and Annie stepped up. Did real good with the twins while she was unavailable. You're here now so they could take that break before Annie has their baby."

It was nice of his brother not to make him feel more regret than he did. "I'll have to check with Bree, but I'd like for Trey to meet Max, and you too."

Wyatt patted him on the shoulder. "Max will be thrilled to find out he has a cousin, and one that's close by. I'll get you contact info for mine and Caleb's attorney that worked out when he adopted Chloe, Annie's girl. Handled Sierra adopting my Max too. Anyway, we're all beginners at parenting. But letting the mom lead is a start. How do you think Bree's going to add into the mix?"

"Not sure. Not getting a lawyer just yet. No need." Responsibility for someone else wasn't his strong suit, as he'd proved more than once. He'd totaled his truck in high school right after getting his license, and his friend at the time still had a slight limp because of it. Responsibility and commitment weren't his forte.

"You sure? I've found it's best to have one before needed."

Gage wondered why the Galloways, his family, were so tight with lawyers. He wouldn't be here if Dad's will hadn't had a clause that each of them had to be involved in the farm for their full inheritance.

"Bree's a great woman. We were inseparable in high school, if you remember. Mainly, I saw concern there after she gave me the truth, with how I would take her not telling me and probably wondering what happens next. I'm confident he is well cared for, and that helps a lot. He was born early and had to have heart surgery, and she made it through all of that."

Wyatt stepped away toward where his crew had halted work. "We've had our challenges, but having a sick child? I can't imagine. This is a lot. Look, I gotta get on this fence, get back to it." He held out his hand and Gage shook it. "Welcome to the daddy club. You're in for a treat."

Gage swallowed as Wyatt's back retreated. He wasn't so sure. Being a father was going to be a new adventure for him. He'd been out of touch with Bree, off the grid even, and they'd both gone on with their lives separately. Hopefully, she'd be reasonable with letting him see Trey and be an influence in his homelife even. He couldn't imagine she had much to offer in financial terms. Not that money mattered more than love, but he wanted Trey to have the most, to cover his needs and to enjoy all the opportunities the world had to offer. Bree would welcome him in that regard, surely, wouldn't she?

He untied Louise from the tree and climbed up into her saddle. One family member knew about Trey, so it was a start.

Louise took off at a run and he let his mind wander. How were he and Bree going to navigate co-parenting, as she called it? An ache in his gut surprised him. A boy needed two parents. But what he really needed was two parents who loved him and each other. He couldn't give that to Trey, but he'd do his best to cover everything else.

Bree sure looked cute in that sweater-jacket thing though.

Where had that come from?

She definitely would be someone he'd look forward to seeing when he was with Trey. He needed to count his blessings.

# Chapter 6

Bree walked up to the museum as the oranges and pink hues of the morning sky shone behind the beloved structure. She'd always thought it looked like the house in her Hansel and Gretel storybook. Yellow mums spilling over their pots anchored each end of the steps. She pressed her key into the doorknob, and the push made the old door with its frosted glass creak, and then it swung open.

The door had already been unlocked and she wasn't alone. "What a beautiful day," Bree said.

"The leaves are supposed to be turning gorgeous colors this year, and they're already starting." Dad's cousin Jo, who was close to her, looked up from where she fussed with the arrangement of the items in a display. "Pretty leaves and sunny weather are on God's agenda for festival weekend, let's hope."

"Guess I can check that one off the festival to-do list," Bree said, setting her satchel of work down, unable to resist white-knuckling her iPhone. "You know how important the weather is to the attendance numbers."

She shuddered and scrolled down through her endless duties as the Dale Murphy Museum's director and host of the annual festival named after the star. "How will I ever get everything done?"

"That's why I came, Breezy." No point in asking her not to use her pet name. "What can I do to help?"

She continued looking at her digital to-do list. "Why didn't you warn me you were coming? I mean, Trey's going to be so excited."

"Why would you think I'd break tradition? I'll help you with him or do whatever else you put in front of me. And if you'd rather not have me underfoot, my friend, Elizabeth saved me a room at her new bed and breakfast."

Bree dragged her gaze from the small screen and glanced around the gift shop, imagining how it looked to visitors. For once, she took the time to soak in the ambiance of its antique lace curtains at the windows, and oak trim that was characteristic of the Queen Ann-style structure. It had been the former home of one of Fair Creek's wealthiest residents, who had donated it years ago to get the tax write-off after their great-grandmother had formed a nonprofit.

Above the fireplace, a gigantic, framed photo of Fair Creek High School classmates, including both of her parents, along with Dale Murphy, drew her attention. After graduation, the woman had gone from a local star, featured at the Indiana State Fair, to worldwide fame. She had become an iconic movie star, then died young in a crash. Every year, her fans worldwide made the pilgrimage to Fair Creek for the anniversary of her death.

"Your mother always said if Dale Murphy had to die, September was the best month to do it…from a festival standpoint, I mean."

Bree tucked her phone away and strolled across the tapestry rug covering the hardwood floor. She reached a glass case, opened the box on top, and started removing painted Christmas ornaments of historic Fair Creek, with vintage Dale Murphy images.

"Mom thought nothing surpassed the beauty of autumn in Indiana," Bree said, her fingers lingering as she touched the smooth, decorative glass bulbs. Her dad hadn't been as involved in her life. An understatement she didn't dwell on. "It doesn't seem possible she died when Trey was two. She almost seems alive when I'm here." She sighed.

Her cousin came over and patted her shoulder. "I feel the same," she said, enveloping Bree in a quick hug.

Jo helped Mom run the museum. The two of them had been friends with Dale Murphy, and Bree had told her much about their schoolgirl shenanigans. These days, Jo's role had been cut back, and she mostly shared her memories with visitors. Bree had been making the business decisions for a few years before her mother died, and Jo had maintained it until Bree could take it over six months ago.

Lately, Bree had opted out of showing her cousin the museum's anemic bank account. Since they were short on money, she was opening the museum's cavernous upstairs as a quasi-bed and breakfast this year, just for festival visitors, only open during the weekend event. She wasn't making breakfast either. Next to the section walled off as Bree and Trey's apartment, she'd made up three decent-sized bedrooms to offer to the public. There'd been a shared bath and a half, and they'd been registered for rent this weekend for over six months.

It was all going to be a lot of work, and she squared her shoulders at the thought. She would do whatever it took to keep this place going. She'd always hoped to have other reasons people came to town at other times too. So many plans. So little time, money, or manpower.

The two of them fell into silence as they worked, instinctively knowing what needed done after all these years. The time went quickly, and the noon whistle rang, startling Bree.

Jo stopped arranging all the hangers just so and looked up. "When's my little pumpkin, Trey, coming?"

"I'm sorry. Not knowing your plans, I made arrangements for him to play over at a friend's after his preschool class ended."

"That's perfectly fine. I'll see him soon. I packed a little lunch for us and stashed it in the refrigerator in the break nook. I'll put all of these history books on this table into an arrangement to make them more enticing. I've got quotes from some on poster board."

Her cousin left and returned with a flowered bag that was insulated for each of them. Hers held a baggie of Triscuits and cheese sticks, her favorite comfort meal.

"How do you do it? Know just what I need, before I even am aware? You really do have a good retail mind too. I'm grateful you've come." Bree smiled. Her cousin hadn't had children and had been like a second mom to her.

"Oh, I almost forgot." Jo handed Bree a newspaper she'd stashed behind a counter. The pages were opened to the middle section. "Since we're both moping a little bit anyway over lost family members, take a look at this . . ."

Bree's eyes landed on a headline Jo pointed to from a little free paper distributed in surrounding towns. She read aloud. "Museum festival may be history," then skimmed down until she found Fair Creek identified, as expected. That was all she needed to see. She hurled the newspaper in the direction of the house's fireplace. It still had its original black wrought-iron tools to stoke a fire—the real thing that had come with the house, not a chintzy electric one.

Her throw fell short, and she dawdled, munching on her crackers and cheese, taking her time going over to finish the job.

"How dare a reporter, who's obviously never been here, print those things." Bree swallowed the last bite and stomped around the room, careful to avoid knocking over a lamp on a table she'd gotten out for the weekend only, which had come from Dale's childhood home. "I'll sue for defamation. Or is it libel?" She didn't know and she didn't care. What difference did it make?

The guy was wrong.

Jo pointed at the papers that had separated and splashed all over the floor, as though Bree were Trey's age. "You pick that up. There's still a woman back in the exhibits. Behave."

"What? There is?"

"She's from Arkansas, came in early. Requested some alone time to look at all those photos that are loose in the back. You know how family history buffs like to sort through them."

One visitor all day, and it was now four o'clock, just an hour before closing. Bree hung her head and searched out the scattered pages. It wasn't as though the fireplace would be used. Thanks to the museum's Historic Registry designation, safety was top priority. No fires allowed. Putting it into the trash where someone might see it rubbed her the wrong way. She stuffed it into her satchel to destroy at home.

"Well, I'm glad to see the article," Bree said, lifting her chin. "Makes me more determined than ever."

"That's my girl. Oh, I meant to ask you something. Elizabeth, and others, I guess, have seen you with one of the Galloways. They say he's a nice-looking man."

Bree pulled in a full breath. Jo had everything to qualify as a card-carrying matchmaker, and also knew her biggest secret. But it was no longer a secret, and she wasn't totally sure how she felt about that.

There was no sense trying to cover it up. "Gage Galloway."

"Really. Trey's dad, then."

Bree nodded.

Jo didn't make a move, which was notable in itself. She normally fluttered around like Aunt Bee on the "Andy Griffith" TV show reruns they watched together. "Oh, I just wondered. That's all." She picked up a dust rag and tended to some antique teacups from Dale's grandmother's home. "I don't want to pry, but does he know?"

She hated the invasion of privacy, but it was no use pretending she didn't comprehend. "He does now."

"I wondered, would you ever consider dating him? I mean, that seems like it would be so good for Trey. That is, if you were interested, of course."

Bree pulled out a list of volunteers who were working the festival hours, studying it with obvious concentration. "We're both upset about how Trey's life has started out, without having two parents. I don't honestly know if we'd date. Haven't spent much time thinking about it." She hoped her nose wouldn't grow as she studied the names on the paper she had practically memorized, wondering who might respond to a little arm twisting to fill in the gaps Ted Mitchell and crew couldn't. "He said it's great that we're friends, good for Trey."

"Well, circumstances change. People can surprise you."

Bree wasn't so sure. Gage had never been wishy-washy about anything. Not ever had he flip-flopped once. Besides, she thought to herself, if there was any cliché historians knew, it was that "Those who don't know history are destined to repeat it." Bree knew her history with Gage. They were wonderful friends, and it would be best to remember that he had made no attempt to reach out to her in these past several years.

"Trey's heart condition was so hard," Bree said. "It taught me that my boy needs a mom to always be there for him, just in case anything else would happen." She'd avoided dating because it would take time away from him.

The doctor had assured her that Trey was "good as new," but you couldn't trust anything in life. A newborn baby having a heart condition changed the way she viewed everything.

Jo put down her dust rag. "Oh, I meant to tell you, I got the out-of-town newspaper courtesy of…oh I forget his name, but he's in the coffee group at Delaney's."

One of the older men hated the festival and didn't want visitors to come. He was probably one who marked off all of his yard near the street so no visitors could park their cars there.

Finished gathering the pages, Bree stacked them together and handed them to Jo, who shoved them back at her.

"I'm going to get some newspapers at Elizabeth's when you're done. Somebody bought that dish from my online auction store, and I left my wrapping stuff at home. But aren't you curious about the details in that? You barely read any of it."

Not really, she wasn't. The tightness in the pit of her stomach told her everything she needed to know. "Congratulations on your sale."

Jo smiled. "I got the bowl at an estate auction in a box of stuff for $10 and sold it for $50. Now, read me that article."

Jo wasn't going to take no for an answer, so keeping her voice low, Bree read aloud, "In its 34th year, the fan base has dwindled for the small-town museum's claim to fame, its native daughter Dale Murphy. Many striking artifacts remain and have drawn crowds to walk the streets of Murphy's quaint hometown and to see her gravesite. But attendance numbers bottomed out last year . . ."

The lump in Bree's throat made it impossible to continue. She lowered the paper. "I sent national press releases hoping for positive coverage. An epic fail."

The bell on the front door jangled, and Bree shook away the thoughts. "Maybe we can boost our visitor numbers for the day." She plastered on a smile.

"That's the spirit. I'd better head upstairs. Might start some comfort food." Jo tucked the newspaper under her arm. "Wouldn't want something to happen to this, for it to catch fire or anything."

"Oh, the horrors."

"It's part of history, like you're always preaching about. Maybe one day we'll laugh at how wrong the writer was, once the museum's rebounded. Now, go see who's here." Jo started up the stairs. "I don't want to cook. I brought some items to auction off, and I'll list them on my store. Maybe I'm on a roll."

Bree started off toward the entrance, shaking her head. She was always inspired by her cousin's positive attitude. She vowed to get herself up to speed and tackle her to-do list. In a few days—ready or not—that bell above her door would be ringing nonstop.

At least she hoped so.

# Chapter 7

Gage looked out the window of the office in the barn at Galloway Sons Farm, past the horse training arena to the fields of crops. The cushy chair he'd sunk into after the chores wasn't helping him keep his focus on the figures on feed prices and a farm magazine with tilling tips that lay spread open across his desk. The urge to yawn sprung up, and he clamped his mouth down until the sensation passed. Forcing his gaze back to the page of numbers, the urge to yawn surprised him again, and when his mouth opened wide, he moved his hand over to hide it, like he was wiping the coffee away from his lips.

"Farm life wearing you down a bit?" Leo's desk was several yards away but too close for Gage's comfort. They'd been up at the crack of dawn to feed and care for the animals, and it was too much togetherness.

"Not hardly. You haven't seen tough times until you've been out with Marines stationed overseas."

Leo closed his laptop and leaned back so far in his desk chair that matched Gage's, he was partially reclined. "You'll get on to the routine."

Sharing personal information had never been Gage's strong suit. But he couldn't have his brother thinking he'd gone soft. "Didn't sleep that great last night."

"I see." Leo scratched his chin. "Stumbling into being a dad can keep you awake tossing and turning. Don't ask me how I know."

Gage flinched inwardly. The intuition the brothers shared about one another would take some getting used to. But Leo understood unexpected fatherhood. In May he'd married Kristin Barclay, his best friend's little sister. He'd adopted three babies Kristin had conceived from she and her late ex-husband's frozen embryos.

"How're you managing with three babies? You know that old saying, people make plans, God laughs? Both of us could have been voted most unlikely to have kids."

"It's crazy, honestly. Signing the adoption papers to make Bailey, Sarah, and Keith my kids was the honor of my life. I mean, besides marrying Kristin."

"Wow. I'm trying to absorb I'm the dad of a five-year-old. I've missed so much."

"You missed a whole lot of diapers, and a fair number of sleep-interrupted nights," Leo said with a chuckle. "But seriously, family is so important to us, and to the extended community of Fair Creek as a whole, that you'll never be going it alone. We're here for you."

He wasn't even sure if he was staying in Fair Creek for the long haul. "I'm not going to lie. I'm jealous that you and Kristin are raising your family together, from the beginning. My actions caused Trey's foundation to be lacking. Not sure how, but I'll spend the rest of my life trying to make it up to him."

"To maybe state the obvious, is there a possibility you'd get together with his mom? Bree's one of the army of volunteers we have coming in to help with the triplets. She's a real sweetheart."

He'd asked himself that question over and over last night as he tossed and turned. "There are so many mixed emotions. I love her as my best friend. I've asked God to forgive me because I hadn't been honest with myself at the time about some romantic thoughts. Something in me is angry I've missed so much. With his heart condition, I could have lost him before I'd met him or even known he existed." Gage swallowed, unable to go on.

"But you didn't. Just maybe think it over. Follow God's leading. Really listen deep inside. That's always saved me. Now, I'd better get back to work. I've got mouths to feed."

The look on Leo's face said there was nothing he would rather do than have three kids. His smile stretched across his face and lit up his eyes.

Seriously mind-blowing. "Any ideas on what to bring to a park date with a picnic, Mr. Dad?"

"That's not where we're at currently, since I'm learning to

chase down pacifiers."

His heart sank. If he wanted this to be really special, he needed to put in some effort. Trey deserved the best childhood, and if he had to research what that involved, he would. That thought perked him up. He might not have what some dads had, but he could dig up information like nobody's business.

The rest of the morning dragged, and he concentrated on his tasks, with seeing Trey and Bree as his rewards at the end of the day. Occasionally, he'd sneak in a quick surf through parenting tips.

He didn't even recognize himself.

"Let's go get some grub." Leo stood and angled his large frame toward the office doorway. "But first, I'll show you a side barn where there are all kinds of ways to entertain kids. Maybe you can borrow something."

Gage jumped out of his chair and snagged his cowboy hat on the way. "Now you're talking."

Leo led the way to a low shed that almost looked like one of the "she sheds" he had written a story about, only four times larger. The bright-teal painted door, its edge trimmed in white, opened into a recreational mecca. A huge pool table with big drop-down pockets stretched across one side. A table game with flippers, like a hockey game for two, and arcade games filled one corner. None of this would help, but in the future, he'd bring Trey here.

He stepped up his pace. Maybe he'd skip lunch and go to the tractor supply store and find something? Did Fair Creek have a sporting goods place? Near the back wall, Leo pulled a string on a ceiling fan that started spinning and light flooded the area. A bucket in a corner overflowed with basketballs and lightweight plastic balls in bright colors.

Leo plucked one of the Frisbees hanging on a nail. "You're going to be fine. The Galloway Foundation we formed after Dad died invested in a major park playground upgrade, added some slides with climbing places for smaller kids, and put down tire rubber for safety. The family meets there to let the bigger kids burn off excess energy. But it's a good idea to take some things, to let your boy know you're up for fun."

Gage's chest tightened at the notion that he had a boy. He wasn't sure how he himself had fun, let alone what a five-year-old's idea would be.

Once Gage had stocked a bag with the Frisbee and a few items, he stowed it in his truck and joined Leo, Wyatt, and the workers for lunch at the main house. He didn't add anything to their conversation or go back for seconds on the tasty sloppy joes and scalloped potatoes from Delaney's Diner. A knot formed in his stomach over his after-work plans.

The afternoon flew by, and he was pulling up to the Fair Creek Park, hands white-knuckled on the wheel. What was his problem? A child wouldn't be that hard to get along with. His mom would help too. Bree being there brought other worries. Close as they were, they had some real differences. He'd brought some things for entertainment partly because she had a high need for activity. She went all in with whatever she did. Sometimes, she seemed almost like too much.

He found the vehicle she'd told him to look for, and he parked beside hers. Trey came running over, with Bree coming at a fast clip carting the biggest picnic basket he'd ever seen, before he could unload what he'd brought to contribute.

"Hi, Daddy!"

Arms stretched around his legs in a bear hug. He stooped down and gave a quick squeeze around the boy's shoulders, then stood.

"Hey, buddy. Good to see you."

The child stepped back and looked up. "Mommy said I could play on the slide. She brought strawberry Jell-O monsters. They're my favorite."

"Are they scary?"

The little boy did everything but roll his eyes. "No. I love to eat 'em."

Gage looked at Bree. Her blue eyes, the shade of the Pacific Ocean, held extra sparkle. She'd done something with her hair that made it exceptionally shiny. "He's been keyed up all day for this." Her delicate throat showed her take a deep gulp.

He furrowed his brow. She'd parented their child when he hadn't known Trey existed, and now he came in like he was Santa Clause. It didn't seem fair. Gage leaned over to reach for the basket handle and caught a whiff of her clean scent with a tint of butter maybe? "May I?" When she nodded, he brushed a quick peck on her cheek before taking the basket from her. Awareness that Trey watched his every move lanced through him. He pretended to let the basket almost drop to the ground. Glancing at Trey, Gage said, "Those monsters must be heavy."

A giggle erupted from the little boy. "It's just food." He doubled over and giggled more.

Bree patted Trey's back. "Be careful of the corn on the cob, Gage. It's wrapped good in foil. Honey, your daddy always made me laugh when we were best friends."

Trey stood to his full height. "He did?"

Her expression aimed at Trey was more than just a simple look. Their eyes met. "Sometimes, it seemed like all we did was laugh when we were together. Come on, sweetie. While I lay out the food, you can go play."

Maybe he hadn't been there for the heavy lifting, but going forward, he would make things as smooth as possible. The activities he'd brought would stay in the truck until he got her approval. "Good idea. That noise is my stomach grumbling with hunger, so we better let your mom do her thing."

Gage headed toward a picnic table in a sunny spot. When she grazed her hand on his elbow and steered him to a flat, grassy spot under the shade, he fell into line.

Working as equals would take practice, and he tamped down his annoyance. What difference did it make if he chose the spot that appealed to him anyway?

After they'd gone a few steps, Bree directed her comments to him but made sure their son overheard. "Trey's a big boy and plays on the equipment on his own. But I stay close by to keep an eye on him, and it's still bright so I keep him out of the sun."

The tightness in his shoulders loosened. She hadn't been controlling him for no reason. There were so many things to factor in with kids, things he knew nothing about, all the more reason to keep the boy in his natural environment. Even shared custody seemed like a bad idea. The one person he'd ever been responsible for, his junior colleague while they were embedded with the service men and women, ended in tragedy.

They reached a place perfectly situated to her specifications, in the shade and close to the monkey bars. Trey ran to the slide. Bree yanked a blanket from her basket and shook it out over the ground, then magically, from out of nowhere, plates, silverware, and all sorts of items landed onto it.

Snapping out of his trance, he moved toward her. "You were always the organized one, but this is seriously amazing."

She beamed up at him as her fingers reached for a plastic container and arranged it on the blanket. "I hope you like deviled eggs. Since it's just me and Trey, he likes some foods most kids might not eat."

He had no basis for comparison. "Sure do, but I'll warn you, my mom's will be hard to top."

She removed another stack of containers, and watermelon shone through one, and some kind of pie. "Well, it's not a competition, although 4H judges have given me Best of Show in several categories."

Wanting to help, he reached in for a small bucket of chicken, which he hopefully couldn't do damage to. "No fair trying to use ancient history."

Every few seconds, she'd take her eyes off him and glance over toward the playground equipment, without skipping a beat. "Oh, that's where you're wrong, city boy. There's 4H for adults."

"I'll be finding my farm boy roots, now that I'm back, and hopefully, you'll be part of that."

She removed the lid on a container of Jell-O portions shaped like little blue and red monsters and held it up. "Time to eat monsters, Trey!"

Out of the corner of his eye, the little boy moved from the landing he stood on and entered the top of the slide, coming down with a swoosh.

Bree came over close enough for him to see the wheat-colored flecks in her blue eyes he'd always admired. "The farm ways will come back to you. It took me a bit to catch on again when I returned. But you'll have me to help."

The warmth in his chest came into full bloom. Too bad she was just talking about them being parents together. Wasn't she?

He lifted his hat and wiped his forehead with his arm, then replaced it. "Good. Because I can be a slow learner at times."

Trey growled, startling him, unaware the boy had come up and stood beside them. "Can I have a monster, Mommy?"

She held the container over the boy's head. "Look at your hands." The child showed his palms up and then down, like it was a familiar routine, and the ground-in dirt probably was too.

Bree directed Trey to bring her the bottled water and washcloth propped beside the basket. "Would you mind?" She handed the Jell-O treats to Gage.

She stooped down, uncapped the bottle, wetted the washcloth, and rubbed it on the small bar of soap tucked inside. Scrubbing the boy's hands, she looked up at Gage. "I'm not crazy about hand sanitizer on delicate skin."

It seemed she'd thought of everything. His head spun with all the details. "You're a lucky little boy, Trey. You've got a very special mommy." And he surprised himself by how much he meant it. The circumstances had been all wrong, but Bree was a special woman and the perfect one to care for Trey. He could see that in everything she did and how they reacted—so far, anyway.

Once the youngest of their threesome was seated, Bree nodded to Trey, nudging him on. The boy intertwined his tiny fingers in front of his face, bowed his head, and started with "God is good. God is great…" At his sweet, solid voice, a lump formed in Gage's throat. Trey didn't go further.

Bree's voice touched him almost as much. "And we thank him for our food." Mother and son finished off the rest of the simple offering of grace together.

Gage swallowed. Bree shouldn't have that impact on him, especially when his hurt of what she'd done lingered. Maybe he really could get past it eventually? If he could forgive, Trey would be better off for it, and Gage likely would be too.

Bree handed out bright-yellow, orange, and blue plates with dividers in them. She let Gage go first, and the scent of the breading on the fried chicken breast he chose filled his nose. The tension of everything being new and how it would go must have tamped down how hungry he was.

He waited for Bree to help Trey with the drumstick he wanted, to put a piece on her own plate, and then for the same process with the bright-red, juicy watermelon, the corn on the cob, and baked beans.

They ate in silence. He couldn't remember watermelon so sweet, or corn kernels the perfect texture, and when butter dripped on his chin, a napkin that said "Happy Summer" sopped it up.

Bree made eye contact and smiled. "Don't worry. I know it's not summer anymore, but those were left over, and they fit my mood."

A train whistle filled the air, in addition to the clanking of its cars running along the track as it snaked through the park.

Trey jumped up and almost tipped over his plate that rested on the blanket. "The train! The train!"

"I'd forgotten about that coming along every night. Want to go a little closer?" He looked at Bree. "Would it be okay? I don't want to spoil his supper."

She eyed the child's plate, with the watermelon mostly gone, the chicken bone picked clean, and some nibbles missing from the corn cob. "Sure, you can. That's about the best Trey does with a meal."

Gage registered again how little he knew about kids, including Trey's eating habits. He started toward the gazebo, which was nearer to the tracks but still safe. A small hand slipped into his and he lightly clasped on, his large hand covering his. Making his steps shorter as they walked along, his heart swelled in his chest, an unfamiliar sensation. Emotions had not been a factor in his life, for the most part. His journalism writings conveyed feelings and had earned him a Pulitzer, but this was different, like it was coming from a different place in him, not the compartment for empathy for what others were going through.

They reached the gazebo, and Gage lifted the boy's lightweight, compact body up onto the bench to stand on so he could see better. The train noise made it difficult to speak, so the two of them just watched, and when Trey looked up, flashed a wide smile, and clapped his hands with glee, Gage let out a laugh and smiled just as big.

It was a long train, just as it had been when he'd been growing up. It flitted through his mind that he and Bree had spent time in this gazebo and listened to the train just like this. It seemed they'd always been smiling, telling tales about near-misses in driver's ed training with their favorite teacher instructing, and mishaps at prom where they'd gone as BFFs. Maybe he should have invited her to come over here?

Nope. Father and son. This was perfect. He had a lot to sort out before anything with someone else.

The caboose went by, and Trey climbed down off the bench. "Yay!" He clapped again, then took Gage's hand, and they walked back, with Trey jumping and skipping, pulling on his hand as they went.

The sunset was trickling down and the evening would be over. They came to their picnic space, and everything was all cleaned up. "I would've helped you clear away."

She smiled. "There wasn't time. Getting dark soon. It's like you to disappear, at times. You ducked into the arcade area when the sophomores were after-prom helpers and it was time to clean up."

He shrugged. "Excitement any way I could get it. That was me." He glanced at the sky streaked with blues, yellow, and oranges—one of the prettiest he'd seen, bar none from any around the world. They had so many memories together, more so than he did with anyone else. Being comfortable with one another was going to be a bonus for Trey.

"Can I go play now?" Trey asked. She nodded. "Bye!" The boy's little legs started pumping him across toward the equipment.

"Woah, not so fast. Come here first."

He obeyed.

Bree got out a tiny lightweight jacket from a different bag, and when Trey came back, she wrestled him into it. The kid was a ball of energy. Wonder where he'd gotten that? Maybe he had more than Gage's overall looks. Maybe they were going to have other traits in common. Both good and bad. He'd do everything in his power to steer Trey away from the downsides, like leaving those who cared most about him to travel to parts unknown. A sinking in his gut landed, making him wonder how that must have felt for his family, for Bree even.

Jacket on, Trey was a little far away on the equipment. There were lights in this nice park, so seeing him wasn't difficult.

"I'm going to go closer and watch him. It'll be his bedtime in not too long. Can you stay a little? You need to go?"

"No place I'd rather be. You're doing a wonderful job with him, if I haven't said that already."

She led the way toward a sort of hidden bench at the side of the playground. "You have. But hearing it'll never get old."

"I'm grateful. From what I've seen of kids, sometimes it's like a rodeo with bucking broncos and clowns rolled into one."

She laughed. "Trey's a child. He has his moments. But for the most part, he's a joy to be around. Now, take that with a grain of salt if you want. As my cousin Jo would say, I am his mom after all."

They arrived at the bench, and she plopped down on one edge, so he took the other. "Don't take this wrong, but I hadn't pictured you as a mother. You seem like a natural though."

Her smile lit up her face and she nodded, then simply turned her gaze to the boy looking like he was related to a trapeze artist, running to the various equipment. "We have a little time, Trey! You don't have to hurry." Her voice was calm, reassuring, and Trey's pace slowed.

Of the few of his colleagues' kids he'd been around, Trey's level of politeness, obedience to his mom, and just overall sweetness rivaled theirs. Some had several siblings, and maybe that played a part in how rambunctious they were. Trey maybe wasn't around other kids that much? And being without a dad… An ache seeped into his chest. Mom, dad, brothers, and a sister were the family unit that had made him who he was. Trey was missing out on so much. Maybe Bree would find someone and there would be half-siblings.

Did he really want Trey not to have full siblings, and was that God's plan? *Lord, take care of Trey, and Bree, too.*

"You're shivering."

Bree rubbed her hands over her arms. "Remembered his jacket and didn't think to pack mine."

Gage slid over to her side of the bench and draped his arm around her shoulder, in a just-friends way. "You've obviously put him first." His fingers grazed her bare shoulder, the skin soft, and her nearness brought to his nose some unusual fruity scent. Mango maybe? He swallowed, mouth dry for some reason.

"Tried to. My mom did the same for me. You wouldn't believe how she went into high gear when she found out I was pregnant. I mean, she hadn't raised me that way. To be having a baby when I wasn't married, not even a boyfriend."

"I'm sorry. I didn't mean for—"

"Stop." Cutting him off, she held up her hand. "I worked through all that long ago, with Mom, through prayer… Trey's a gift. Don't ever apologize to me for him."

"Okay. Point taken. I've enjoyed knowing him in this short time. I can only imagine how you feel." *Shift gears, now.* "So, what do you do in your vast amounts of free time?"

She placed her hand on his forearm. "No, you really can't even imagine, and I just wanted to say that. You have no idea how it hurts to think you missed out on so much, even the dark nights in the hospital after his surgery, and the really, really hard parts. I wouldn't have skipped any of it, and even though I made those calls, was bounced around endlessly trying to reach you,

I'm sorry."

He didn't know how to react to her sincerity. But he was pretty sure saying he forgave her, when he wasn't at all sure that he ever could, was not the right move.

She shifted on the bench and looked over at Trey playing. "Funny you should ask about my off hours. I've become close friends with Kristin, your brother's wife. And I'm on her list of coming by regularly to help take some of the load off of caring for the triplets." She shrugged, her smile wide and reaching to her eyes. "Guess I can't get enough of babies."

"Wow. That's the last thing I expected you to say. Leo did say you'd been hanging around though."

"I can't believe it either, honestly. I've changed, for Trey. But when you're friends with somebody, you do things you might not do. I'm going tomorrow, actually, filling in."

He wondered how he could be a better friend to Bree. A car drove up to the pizza joint at the edge of the park and did an awful job of fitting into the space.

"That guy needs some driver's ed. Remember when I taught you how to parallel park on a downtown Indianapolis street that time?"

"Best life skill lesson ever."

Where had the guy who people could rely on gone? "Friendship is something special, isn't it? I've valued you and have done a terrible job of showing it. Maybe instead of hearing you apologize, I owe you one."

"Lately, I've come to think hurting each other is part of life.

Instead of thinking we won't, maybe it's in the forgiving that real relationships are built." She stood. "I've got to get Trey to bed. Big day at the museum tomorrow, and I can't have him dragging to go to the babysitter."

Gage followed her over to the equipment. Good thing she didn't expect an answer to her idea on forgiving. He sure didn't have one. For a moment, it had been just the two of them, saying whatever came to mind, as they used to.

They came to where Trey crouched at the top of the slide. He slipped down and landed where they waited. "Time to go home," Bree said.

Gage waited for the protests, but the kid was dusty all over, especially his face, under his eyes that were droopy. "You going, Dad?"

Kid didn't pull any punches. "Just you and your mom. My truck's over there." Maybe it was time to show him where he lived. Not sure if that would help the partings or not.

The three of them started moseying toward Bree's car, and once there, Trey went right into the back seat where his mom secured him. Gage gave him a quick hug, motioned goodbye to both, and left.

A couple of minutes later, he was pulling away in his truck. Somehow, a bit of his heart was still riding with them. He'd thought this whole dad thing was going to get easier. But in reality, it was going to get harder. A whole lot harder. He just had a feeling.

# Chapter 8

Bree pulled up to the museum, grateful the morning sun shone on the historic building to help keep her eyes open. The pointed roof was one of the higher in town, and fans always remarked on it. She'd barely slept last night, after getting Trey settled down past his usual bedtime, since he'd chattered so much about their time with Gage. Once her head had finally hit the pillow, the sandman stayed away, and she'd gotten into a deep doze way too close to getting-up time.

A big box full of folded T-shirts sat on a counter. Bree picked up a navy one and shook it out. The festival date and design popped, created by the teen winner at the high school contest.

The little bell above the door jangled, signaling a visitor.

Bree went and hugged Kristin. "How'd you get away? I remember just leaving Trey was hard when he was so little."

Her close friend went to the mantel of the fireplace and set down a bag stuffed with papers poking out of the top. "Leo gave me a spa day from the kiddos, and we're having a date night. First one since the babies. Thought I'd stop in with the publicity posters from last year."

Bree held up a T-shirt. "Very sweet of you, in your precious little free time. We got the first delivery in. Aren't these great?"

Kristin whistled. "Nice, wouldn't be surprised if that art student is going places." The annual high school art contest to pick a design for the shirts had been especially gratifying this year. "That printed out even better than I anticipated."

Bree swayed to fake music as she went over to a counter. "And here's something for the true history buffs among us. Look at this." A purse with the iconic photo of Dale Murphy spread across it, sporting a short handle like the "pocket purses" from the 50s, lay next to some combs and postcards with her image. "When I saw all these in the catalog, I had to have them."

"You've got your finger on the pulse of the customers." Kristin laughed. "So, how'd it go with Gage last night?"

There it was. The real reason Kristin had come, most likely. She had never been one to beat around the bush, as Mom used to say. "Perfectly fine."

"Well, that is loaded with insight. Really, it's me and I want to know. How was it? Being around him, and Trey, with them together."

If she didn't share, Kristin would drag it out of her, and it would put her radar up even more than it already was. "I don't know. How's that for an answer? I've waited for this moment for so long, for Trey to have his dad. So, it's all good."

"That's not what I meant, and you know it. How was Gage, with you?"

"He complimented me on my parenting skills."

"Oh. Well, that's good. But is it what you really wanted to hear?"

The problem with a long-term friend was they knew all your inner thoughts. "I don't know what I wanted." Bree had been left with a hurt in her gut that hadn't let up. Maybe she'd hoped for something…more.

"Well, you know what that TV psychiatrist says."

Grateful for the change of topic, she asked, "Which thing, about facing reality?"

"Nope. You've got to name what you want before you can go for it."

*Lord, help me to want what's best.*

"It's no secret. What's best for my baby. Now that his dad's in the picture, that's going to make all the difference, an answer to prayer."

Two taps on the door stopped her from spilling more as she hustled to open it. There was a big box on the museum porch and another little one propped on the porch railing.

Bree brought them in and ripped open the small one. Clear bags nestled inside were full of stickers of the actor in his cowboy costume from his last movie. "Oh, I forgot all about ordering these." She lifted one up. "Aren't they cool?"

"Yes, but that's not the subject here.

"It most certainly is." She flounced her hand around the room. "My family exists in this building. Mom stood over by that fireplace and announced the first parade. Hmm. Maybe we should frame and put up the photo of that."

"And maybe you shouldn't. Fan surveys say they want more about Dale Murphy herself and not so much about the townspeople."

"Thanks for that. We're in this slump in the first place because the fans haven't always been listened to in the past."

Bree went to the desk where she conducted business and recorded that on the list on her clipboard. "Confirm the parade master, line up press coverage for Saturday. Get the golf carts for our volunteers. What am I forgetting?"

"Did you remind the judges for the Dale Murphy look-alike contest? What about the 50s dance contest? Assuming that one guy is doing the Spooky Murphy Tour again this year, a fan favorite that's building."

Bree felt an appreciation for Kristin's support. She wasn't alone. "Yes. I need to find his name and confirm. Who knew tromping around town at night, telling stories at the actor's grave site, and dropping by the deteriorating school she graduated from would be popular? Wish we had more vendors. There's still a good amount, but we go down a little every year." Vendors attracted the crowd, and the booth fees brought in desperately needed funds.

"Well, it is what it is. You'll come up with something else.

I'd better get going. Put my name down for helping you clean and let's schedule it when I've got volunteers loving on Keith, Bailey, and Sarah." The proud mama objected to calling the trio "the triplets." She said it didn't give them recognition as distinct individuals.

"I'm sure you've got more important things to do than help me clean." She hated housework, which was how the dust had gathered in the first place. "I'll hire someone to come through with a fine-tooth comb." Not that she really would part with hard-earned money to chase away harmless dust bunnies that kept her and Trey company.

"Nope. I'm coming back at some point. You can update me on the Gage status."

Bree opened her mouth to protest, and Kristin held up the palm of her hand, indicating to stop. "Pop psychology aside, don't be afraid to bring what seems impossible and lay it at God's feet." Her words caught in her throat, and she swallowed. "Mine are named Keith, Bailey, and Sarah. Oh, and I can't leave off Leo. Just sayin' I've got enough faith for the both of us."

Kristin's phone rang, and she held up one finger as she picked up. "I understand." She paused for the other person to speak. "That's fine. You've done the right thing. We'll manage. Feel better soon."

Kristin disconnected, and with her phone still in hand, she announced, "Well, Shirley can't take her shift with the babies this evening. Doesn't feel good and has a slight fever."

"There goes your date night."

Kristin headed toward the door, and Bree called out, "Hey, I'll cover for Shirley tonight."

Her friend stopped and waved her hand around the room. "I can't let you do that."

"Consider it payment for the cleaning you'll be doing."

Kristin's eyes held a sparkle that had been missing. "We really do need a date night. I'm so tempted. But Shirley brings her daughter as her helper. I can't leave you alone to fend for yourself."

"Trey will come. He's good with doing the little helper things that will get me through."

The other woman's face lit up. "Well, if you're sure. Seems like the colic or whatever it is that bothers them in the evening is worse."

"No worries. Auntie Bree knows what to do." Mainly, she'd need to fight off baby fever. Holding the little darlings caused a longing with a strength that almost frightened her. The schedule was fixed, and she had volunteered before, just normally with another adult. "I'll see you at 6:00 p.m. Be sure to wear that filmy new blouse you picked up the other day. Leo's eyes will pop."

Kristin's cheeks took on a pink flush. "I can't wait. Thanks."

Alone again in the shop, the empty hangers on the rack from last year's sales called to her. She carried the box of shirts to the counter and began hanging them.

If there was one fund she counted on, it was selling shirts. Fans collected them, and the regulars bought one every year. She just needed something else to draw them in, and maybe with a higher profit margin. Shirts made her only a few dollars, once she covered the cost of the shirt and printing. She picked up her pace. All these shirts wouldn't hang themselves.

What had she gotten herself into by helping with Kristin's babies? She'd always been the supporter and never done the heavy lifting when it came to them.

She didn't need the practice of caring for babies, since she'd never have more of her own. Would she?

# Chapter 9

Gage stood on the front porch of Leo and Kristin's house, with baby cries coming through the door. He didn't know how he'd ended up driving Bree and Trey over here, but her car had acted up. He'd planned to drop them off for Leo to bring home. But he suspected his little family wanted him to join them. So he'd turned around and come back.

He held up his hand to knock. Would anyone inside hear him? Leo had put a bug in his ear that Bree and Trey were caring for his niece and two nephews tonight, nudging him to get involved.

There was still time to walk away down the steps. No one would be the wiser. He gazed at his truck at the top of the driveway, practically calling his name with its bright, shiny red paint. There wasn't a reason he could think of to jump in here. Motherhood had to be the most difficult job ever. The word brought a lump to his throat, an image of his own mom. Lately, he'd gotten to know the mother of his colleague who had passed. At the funeral, he'd seen how broken she was and had made a point to visit her once and call every few weeks.

A cow mooed in the distance, stopping his ruminating. He shook his head clear of the thoughts and rapped his knuckles on the door. Shifting his boots back and forth as he waited, he squelched the desire to sneak away for good. This was all too new. Nothing he'd ever wanted, at least on any conscious level.

The door swung open. His gaze traveled down to Trey standing there. "Daddy!" Small, but surprisingly strong arms gripped him. His son. A lump formed in Gage's throat.

He patted the boy's head. "How've you been, partner?"

The boy swiveled and called into the room. "Mommy, Daddy's here."

"Well, step aside so he can come in, sweetie." Looking past Trey, at the far side of a huge living room, or what people called a great room, Bree sat on the sofa with a baby in each arm. Their open mouths and their wails were clearly the reason he had to strain to hear her.

Trey let go of his grip on Gage's leg and stood back. Gage's chest tightened as he surveyed the room. Another baby sat in some baby chair thing with a brightly colored cloth back and also wailed. How many ways could he say that he didn't belong here, was out of place. Or maybe the sensation was something else. Cold, hard fear.

Too frozen to move, he remained motionless as Trey closed the door, and then his small, warm hand grabbed Gage's and pulled. "Come on." Gage marched into the room before he lost his nerve.

The appropriate words escaped him. "Any ideas on ways to help them stop crying?"

Closer to her now, the strain on Bree's face showed, and words came from clenched teeth and a tense jawline. "I'm trying. Sometimes, it just goes like this. Kristin isn't sure whether they have colic or what. They have a crying jag about this time every evening."

"No wonder Leo sent me here. Traitor."

Her face muscles relaxed, and a smile played on her lips. "You've never liked situations out of your control, have you?"

"Who does?"

"True. But one thing you'll learn is that caring for kids is messy. That's not all bad though."

He stopped short of yelling to be heard, just barely. "Tell me what's good about it?"

"It makes you appreciate the quiet times?" Her shrug said it all.

The baby wails seemed to crescendo.

She tilted her head, leaning so she was centered amid the crying. "Can you try the pacifiers again, sweetie?"

Gage hadn't noticed their son had moved to the farthest edge of the room. Now he jumped up from where he crouched on the floor playing with the toy tractor he'd given him, along with other equipment.

"Trey to the rescue!" He went and gathered up pacifiers from a low table in the center of the room. "Here, baby." Starting with the one in the seat and making his way around to the two in Bree's arms, he expertly filled the babies' mouths with the plastic gadgets.

The din of their wails lessened at each act of mercy Trey performed. "I've written a variation of the phrase 'the silence was deafening' many times but may not have realized what it means until now."

"Better enjoy it while you can. So far, pacies are a temporary fix."

Their little lips latched around their comfort moved in rhythm as they sucked. "You're kidding. Can I bring you anything? A sedative? A nanny to take over for you?"

She giggled, and the sound was better than even the silence. Too bad they were best friends only.

Wait, what was that about?

"Is a glass of water on your list? And grab yourself a root beer while you're at it."

Trey had settled back with his pretend farming. "Root beer!"

His mom coaxed him into adding please.

Pop wasn't good for a growing boy. That much he knew. "Can I persuade you to order milk instead?"

"It's okay for an occasional treat, according to the mommy handbook."

Gage schooled his features away from a frown. "He's done a

man's job with the babies, so it's time for a man's drink then." The grin on Trey's face rewarded his remark and spurred him into heading toward the kitchen cabinet he could peek around and see.

Returning with the drinks, he handed them around. A wail came from the baby in the seat.

"Oh no. We're heading back to purgatory?"

"Brace yourself. I don't know if it's a coincidence or has something to do with them being triplets, but they are often in synch, when I've been here anyway. One will cry, and it's not unusual for all of them to start up."

Not on his watch, they wouldn't. Taking advantage of the nearest coaster on an end table, Gage plopped his drink down. How much harder could this be than calming a puppy one of the soldiers he covered had found as a stray?

Leaning down on his haunches, his fingers seemed too big as he fiddled with the doodad to unstrap Keith, whose name was on his shirt. "Simmer down there. Uncle Gage has you." The cries ratcheted down a notch as pools of blue eyes that seemed huge in the petite, delicate face stared up at him.

He eased the tiny body out of the seat, which weighed more than he expected. A solid chunk this one was. "You're not going to break, are you?"

Keith shut his mouth. The turned-up corners of his mouth encouraged Gage. "You've got the nicest smile."

Bree's two dumplings continued to cry but maybe not so loudly, or maybe two just sounded quieter. "Gage Galloway.

You've been holding out on me. You're good with babies."

Bree hoisted herself off the sofa and seemed to steady herself in place, holding both babies.

"Yay, Daddy!"

Gage opted not to hide his pleasure and grinned at each of his co-conspirators in turn. He held Keith closer, and the baby nuzzled into his shoulder. "As I've told you, I'm full of secrets. We've been apart in what experts say are the greatest years of growth and change, other than the baby years like they're in."

Bree stepped over toward Trey. "Your job makes you a walking dictionary. I don't know about any of that."

They did a bit of a dance around the room, letting the babies look at each other when their paths nearly crossed.

They stood shoulder to shoulder, and he patted Keith's back. Without warning, some milky substance spewed onto him, and his chest felt a sensation of a wet chill.

"Oh, no. Spit up on your pretty cowboy shirt. My bad. I should have given you a burp cloth." She grabbed a rag from a pile of them tossed over the sofa back and tucked it under the baby's mouth.

"That's why your shoulders are covered, Bree. Good to know. Too late for me. Ever heard of a washing machine though? Modern magic, there."

The scent wasn't strong but not great either. Her voice came out almost as a whisper, "Hey, Bailey's asleep. Maybe tummy trouble had something to do with her crying after all."

The baby's eyes were closed, her lashes lying across her

cheeks. "Guess I'm not so well researched. I thought if they were fed and dry, you were good to go."

"Go back to your research, Gage. They're little people, complex like every human. If you're fed and clothed, is that all you need?"

"Not even close." Their eyes locked, so near he could see the gold flecks, the color of wheat, in her blue eyes. How had he never noticed them before?

"What do you want, Gage?"

When in doubt, answer with a question. In a hushed tone, not to wake them, he said, "Never were one much for small talk, were you?" He smiled and reached for his own drink, took another swallow. "This root beer hits the spot. That's for sure. Both of yours have fallen asleep."

A flicker of emotion Gage couldn't identify entered her eyes and faded. "I said they respond in threes, sometimes. Let's go put them down."

"Really? Not sure I can handle them cranking it back up."

"They've crossed over into dreamland and should be fine. Follow me."

He trailed her down a hallway. Once in the bedroom, the late-evening sun peeked out beneath the darkening blinds, helping to see in the small room. Three cribs lined the far wall, with each child's name written in script on little wooden signs above them. Following Bree's lead, Gage moved in slow, tiny motions, until all the adorable slumbering bodies were on their backs. A baby monitor on a table beamed as they tiptoed out, and Bree pulled the door behind them.

Once back in the great room, Trey hadn't budged from his spot. Gage selected a place on one end of the sofa, and Bree touched down only for a moment, then leaped up.

"Would you like a snack?"

"Me! Me!" Trey jumped up and down with his hand raised.

Bree smiled and responded to Trey. "I hear you. Let's see what our guest thinks." Her face was still all lit up when she turned back to Gage.

He wasn't sure why being called a guest bothered him, but it did. "I'll go with what the majority wants."

"Well, it's our tradition to have a snack once the babies are down—more like a celebration, really. Sometimes, it takes a lot longer than others to settle them. You've been a big help tonight. Whenever we're coming, I stock up on treats. Let me get my bag."

Leave it to her to think of everything and bring it along. Good thing he'd been good with getting the babies to sleep or he would have felt useless. She left and returned, lugging a large, festive bag decorated with horses and wreaths.

"We've got several choices." She unzipped her tote and began spreading the goods on the coffee table.

"You weren't kidding."

Trey came over and observed her. "These are something you might want to try." She held up a roll of candies in waxed paper.

"Neccos? Great-grandpa used to buy those for us kids, darling."

Trey wrinkled his nose. "What's that? Chocolate's my favorite."

He picked up a bite-sized one, and Gage noted it said "fun sized" on the bag. He must really be out of it when it came to candy. All sizes were fun for him.

Bree grinned. "I'm glad you asked about these, just like Mommy teaches you, to be open-minded."

Gage looked in time to see Trey crumple his mini candy bar's wrapper and scarf it down. Bree unwrapped the candies and held out one little pale disk. "Necco Wafers were invented by a man named Oliver Chase who came over from England. During the Civil War, or The War Between the States, the Union soldiers carried them with them."

"Cool!" The boy took s Necco, chewed, and swallowed. "Can I have another candy bar?"

He reached for a little bar, and Bree nodded her approval. "Here's something you may like better: a box of Cracker Jacks. I loved these as a kid when my mom, your Grandma Murphy, took me to see the Reds in Cincinnati."

She held up the familiar box, and Gage wondered when he had seen one last. Maybe when he was about Trey's age? His mouth watered for the caramel coated popcorn. Whenever it was, the candy had made a lasting impression.

"You know what I loved about Cracker Jacks when I was a kid, Trey?"

The boy looked up at him with those big brown eyes. "You ate these? Wow, they must be really old."

"Trey!" Bree's tone wasn't severe, and the corners of her mouth twitched as if she might smile.

She handed a little box to Gage, and he responded to Trey. "I am old, compared to you. This says, 'prize inside.' When I was your age, I couldn't wait to find what little trinkets they put inside."

Trey let Bree open the box for him. "Wow!" He started digging through the popcorn. A couple of pieces dropped on the wood floor as she placed a dish under the box to catch strays.

Gage's fingers were so much bigger than the last time he tried this. He didn't want the sticky snacks to land all over the floor. Bree handed him a dish. "Honestly, you two. Why can't you be like me and eat your way along until you find the prize?" She giggled, and it was a pretty great sound. When had it stopped being okay to just laugh together and call it friendship?

Gage shrugged. "Guess that's a way I'm exercising control. At least I'm not dumping it out to see the prize."

"Look." Trey held up a little wrapped item and managed to rip the covering open. "All I got was a little book."

"Found mine, too." Gage held up a wrapped-up doodad. "Would you like to trade?"

"Yay."

Gage gave him the toy, and Trey released the book into his outstretched palm, giving Gage a little smile before wondering off to go play.

Gage munched a piece. "I've never seen such a big deal made of treats. Pretty sure my mom just threw them in a bowl and we scrambled for them."

"As they say, your mileage varied growing up. With Joe eight years older, I was an only child, to some extent."

"I sometimes forget you have a brother. With five of us, even though there is an age spread, no one was solo for long." He took a handful of popcorn. "I'd forgotten all about these candies."

"History is so important to me, always has been. What better way to open a kid's mind to the past than with candy?"

He swallowed the popcorn and considered her statement. "Oh, right, you were a history nerd. Didn't you try single-handedly to save some old building in town?"

She cocked her head and her blue eyes sparked at him, although in a teasing way. "'Some old building?' There's no such thing. If those walls could've talked, I'm just sayin'. An historic school building made of beautiful architecture deserves to be preserved. Dale Murphy walked those hallowed halls and was in a play on that school stage." She drew the back of her hand across her forehead and flopped onto the back of the sofa in the perfect imitation of a movie star fainting.

"Oh, right, you used to imitate Dale Murphy. Played her part in the school play of her movie, *The Peony of Indiana*."

She batted her eyes at him. "How could you have forgotten?"

"Will you ever find it in your heart to forgive me?"

Bree laughed. "You've never held on to anything. We got into that big fight over your throwing out the T-shirt from our freshman homecoming week."

"I was a senior and heading out to parts unknown. Good riddance."

"I may have dug it out of your wastebasket behind your back.

It's probably here somewhere."

"Talk about ridiculous."

"Fooled you. It's not my job to keep a memory for you that you don't value."

"Then why are you so latched on to the museum, if you don't mind my asking?"

Her eyes sparkled, as if she'd been waiting for this chance. "No one understands. I'm not sure if I want to try to explain since it's natural to me, so why bother? It's not like people change their minds."

"Guess it's a touchy subject. I'd like to know. It's always good to state your position. Never can predict whose eyes might be opened, darling."

"Studying the way things used to be inspires me for the future. There've always been struggles, and each generation finds ways to triumph."

"Hate to admit this, but I can see your point. I think preserving old stuff can be taken too far. But I enjoy hearing your views. You're so passionate, and sometimes that's a rarity."

"Well, there are some historians who support keeping things above people. If land's needed for housing, I'm all for putting it to use. It'd be nice to carry the building to another location, if it's important though."

There was a tap on the outside door and the knob turned. When Leo stepped in, Kristin came right behind. Gage whispered, "Maybe we aren't as far apart as we think." Then he directed a comment to the interlopers, since they'd interrupted a conversation he hadn't been ready to end. "What? You guys back already?"

Kristin hooked her hand into the crook of Leo's elbow. "We've had a wonderful break. Didn't want to make Trey too late for bed and it's 8 o'clock already. Bailey, Keith, and Sarah sleeping?" She headed toward the hallway without waiting for an answer.

Leo asked Trey, "How's the farming going, buddy?"

Gage couldn't believe how much his brother had changed from the days when his full attention stayed on the paintbrush in his hand.

"I'm hauling corn." The tractor pulled a little wagon behind it, a miniature version of the real thing. He loaded real corn kernels from the field in the back.

"Good job." Leo turned to Gage and Bree. "Don't let Kristin fool you, all she talked about was the kids and how they might be getting along. I held her off from calling. Finally decided to call it a night."

Bree gave Gage warning look. "Piece of cake. Next time, let her check, and we'll put her mind at ease so you get a longer night out."

Leo yawned so big he covered his hand to stifle it. "Those three don't sleep through, and last night they wanted to play after their feeding. I'd be happy to be in bed before Trey here."

It all sounded so cozy. Going home by himself didn't sound as attractive anymore. What was the matter with him?

"Put your toys in the carrier, Trey." Bree slipped her feet into her shoes and had begun packing her snacks away about the time

Kristin returned.

"Sometimes, I just like to watch them breathe. Thank you for taking such good care of them."

He stood up, and since Bree had set the tone, Gage played along. "It was nothing. Call on us again, anytime."

Leo stared at him and shook his head. "You mean it? Oh, and thanks for staying and giving Trey and Bree a ride home."

"Emphasis on 'us,' not just me, I hope that's understood. Driving them will be my pleasure."

Bree came up beside him with Trey, both carrying their things in colorful, sturdy totes, as he had become accustomed to seeing them with.

After saying their goodbyes, the three of them stepped onto the porch as the door shut behind them.

Trey pointed overhead. "The moon!"

At the same time, Gage and Bree looked at the orangish, pinkish giant ball in the sky.

She patted their son's shoulder. "That's the prettiest one yet." Her comment was hushed and still clear in the stillness of the night. "We do this every night." She directed her comment to him.

The simple beauty of the moment put a lump in his throat for some reason. "I'd have to agree. Maybe I'd better start doing this myself."

She caught his eye and held his gaze. "You really think so, after all the places you've been?"

"I'd stake my life on it."

"You were always dramatic." The sparkle in her eye and her grin conveyed she didn't mind.

"I had to carry on enough for the both of us." He used to be bothered by how unemotional she was, especially compared to the women he'd known, including his own mother. She never let her feelings show. But he'd come to appreciate her steadiness.

Were they really parked here on a porch in the middle of farm country staring at the moon and he wasn't bored, not at all?

Trey yawned. "We better get you home, buddy. Morning comes early tomorrow." They moved toward his truck. The car seat was still there. "I'll help with the door..." But Trey had climbed into the vehicle by himself.

Maybe Gage's idea that Trey always cooperated wasn't true. But then, the kid got his independent spirit from somebody, so he couldn't complain. He hoped he was up for the challenge.

# Chapter 10

Gage reached over the truck seat to help secure Trey in, where he sat in the back seat.

"I can do it myself, Daddy."

Safety had been important to him since the car accident. For a minute, he was thrown back to that time. What if he got this wrong? "I want to check everything's okay, Trey."

Under protest, Gage reached over to be sure the seatbelt had clicked into its holder. A whiff of caramel and soap combined with the grime of the day floated up. He gave Trey's hand a pat and shut the car door.

With Bree getting a head start on him, she wasn't feeling as inept as he was.

Moving around to the driver's seat, a prayer for wisdom went up. He'd never planned for this, and yet in his gut, he wouldn't have wanted to miss any of it. He just hoped he didn't mess it up.

Once behind the wheel, he glanced over at Bree where she relaxed against the seat. "You didn't have to do this, Gage. But it's so nice that you decided to be with us tonight. I wouldn't be truthful if I said that I haven't thought of what it would be like to have the whole minivan and family together dream."

He reached over and linked hands with her, then put both hands on the wheel. "I might not have wanted this. I appreciate you're letting me into your life, to Trey's life. There really is not one without the other, is there? You two are a team."

"I'm glad you see that. No, there isn't. We'll be attached to one another through Trey for the rest of our lives."

What did he say to that? He'd never taken care of a guppy, let alone a child. He wanted their relationship to be built on trust from here on out. "I may take a little while to get used to things. It's all pretty new to me."

He started the engine and then drove away. Maybe this hadn't been such a good idea.

Silence reigned as the moon shed an eerie glow over the cornstalks on one side of the road and soybeans on the other. Again, he couldn't believe the beauty and how well it held up as compared to all the places he'd traveled. This sight, with the people he loved, exceeded experiences at the pyramids, the wonders of the world in Athens, and even the Middle East. Nothing compared to this Midwest fall landscape.

They came up to the edge of town. "It's happening. Ready or not." Bree gestured toward an open area on a side street where rows of golf carts were parked, each four carts deep.

"A golf cart invasion?"

"The Dale Murphy Festival, silly. People rent those so they can get around in the crowds. At least I hope there'll be lots of people. My stomach is churning now."

"Adulting isn't for the wimps, huh? When we were kids, it was all fun and games."

"As much as we've stayed the same here, we've also changed. Like everything, I guess. Golf carts were always a thing since I started using one to quickly get to all the places I need covered over the weekend."

Gage glanced in the rearview mirror to check on Trey. The kid's head tilted as it rested on the seat, and his eyes were shut, mouth slightly open. The desire for a worry-free childhood, as every kid's should be, welled up in him. He just wasn't sure how much he would be able to contribute, and he was expected permanently back in DC eventually.

In the semi-darkness of the truck's interior, he caught Bree's eye. "You've sold me. Now I want a golf cart."

"Oh, come on." Her blue eyes sparkled, and he loved how he knew she teased right back when he threw her a line. "Guess it's true what they say, the only difference between men and boys is the number of their vehicles."

"Would it make me look better if I offered to help you for the weekend, put the cart to use?"

She pursed her lips how she did when teasing was over, and something resonated deep inside of him. "Looking good has never been an issue for you, Gage. Not ever."

"So does this mean you won't accept my services, or let me have a golf cart? 'Cause I'll ask Wyatt to cover the farm if you'll have me."

He was in over his head and didn't know what possessed him to offer. He drove through streets of Fair Creek that he hadn't been through in a long while. She didn't seem to mind. Getting to her place would end the intimacy of the truck cab, with just them, the world shut out.

And that would be a very good thing. What was the matter with him?

She studied him, as if she could see his turmoil, maybe? "You've made me an offer I can't refuse. The golf cart order is a done deal, but you won't need your own. You can share mine and Trey's."

He raised his eyebrows. "I like the sound of that, darling."

She turned away to look out the window, but he thought he caught a tinge of pink on her cheeks first. "Look over there!" She spoke softly, but her tone was like a kid seeing a circus for the first time. "Those carnival rides parked in the field are the telltale sign things are really going to happen. They'll move in and set up in town once the streets are closed off Thursday night."

"Enthusiasm really is contagious, like they say. Will I be able to take Trey on some rides, boss?"

"Only if I get to go along."

"Tilt-a-wheel, here we come."

"Nope." She hesitated, and he hid his disappointment. "That's too tame for me. I go for the ones that whiz through the air, preferably upside down some of the time."

"I might need you to hold my hand."

She giggled, a sound he was beginning to savor every time. "That can be arranged."

"Good to know I won't have to haul you over my shoulder like a sack of potatoes to get you away from your weekend duties."

"Are you aware you're starting to sound like a real cowboy who has never left here?"

"Something's going on with my language, if that's what you mean. But I would have taken the farm boy approach if that's what it took."

"Might be worth it for me to stage a resistance just to find out what that's like. But I learned a long time ago that I've got to mix fun in with the work. Actually, having Trey taught me that. I don't want to sell you on parenthood. Only you can do that. But being his mom really is the most lifesaving, most life-affirming thing I've ever experienced."

He wasn't there quite yet. Not even close. One evening or two seeing how parents lived wasn't enough. And that had already overwhelmed him.

She looked at him again, her eyes extra blue, even in the darkness. "Speaking of which, you better get us home. There's my street."

"Guess I got carried away. You don't know how special slow times are until you've experienced the rat race of so many other places in the world."

"What have you done with Gage, the one with the city lights in his dreams his whole life?" She laughed. "Like I told you, I've lived in the city too. But it might be easy for some people to take living around here for granted. Nice you're seeing it with fresh eyes."

He got them home and pulled into her parking space at the side of the museum. They both opened their doors, got out, and walked around to Trey's door.

Gage's mind shifted, being outside the bubble of the car. "I'll carry him in for you." Well, that came out wrong, a little bossy and gruff.

"No, thanks, I'll do it. He's used to me."

Well, ouch. The way she said it couched no debate on the issue.

Would Trey be used to him one day? Or would his mom always be his number one? He wasn't sure how he felt about that or any of this. Fearful, came to mind. Hesitant. Gage opened the vehicle door, and how easily she gathered up the boy took him by surprise. He filled her arms, but he was pretty light weight. And she was not anyone without size of her own that could manage anything that needed to be done, which he'd always admired about her.

"Well, I'd like to open the door for you, at least."

"That'd be great. Grab my keys out of my bag?"

He reached into her bag that she'd slung on one shoulder, easily finding the keys in a side pocket, where she guided him.

They started to walk in silence to the front door. He

appreciated that she wasn't the kind of woman who had to dig around for her keys, although to each his own, as his mother used to say. But Bree was just so capable. That was the word. That seemed like a very good thing, not boring or dull as he might have thought at times when they were younger.

They arrived and he unlocked the door, then tucked her keys back where he'd found them. "Bree Murphy, I want to be just like you when I grow up." He'd spoken more solemnly than he'd intended.

"I don't know. I kind of like you just the way you are."

Without thinking, Gage leaned over and gave her a peck on the cheek, taking him back to the night when they'd said the long goodbye. Bree's soft skin and her scent of soap and strawberries, the last as he got close to her hair, were just the right mix. He stepped away, with some effort, and gave a casual wave.

She called softly, "Thank you for this evening. You don't know how much I needed it, before the crazy starts happening for real."

"Happy to help." More or less, when he wasn't drowning in doubts. "Why don't you let Trey come visit me on the farm in the morning? Tag along for my chores."

He could handle that amount of responsibility, he was pretty sure.

"He'd love that. Preschool isn't every day, so he's free. Can I bring him over around eight o'clock? We're early risers."

"Absolutely. See you then."

He hustled away before he reconsidered.

Not sure how to read the look she gave him, and the slight

wave of her hand, he waited until she'd made it inside and shut the door. He walked down the sidewalk from the museum with a smile on his face, the pleasure of the evening overwhelming him. What would tomorrow bring with Trey and his mommy?

# Chapter 11

Morning came too early when Bree had been up late thinking about what needed to be done at the museum. Her stomach twisted in a knot as she helped Trey to pack his bag to visit Gage.

"You're only going for a day. Your dad's going to show you what he does around the farm."

The kid had carried a blanket around until he went to preschool, and his bag of toys seemed to have replaced that to create his sense of security. He probably felt something like she did, excited and nervous.

"Here, let me help." She took out a tractor. "Now, if you reach in and put the farmer, cow, and horse into that outside pocket, you'll have enough room to get the wagon in."

"Thanks." He hugged her.

"Always happy to assist you. Now, which cereal do you want?" She'd splurged and gotten little packs of cereal boxes so he'd have a variety.

"Not hungry."

If there was one thing she'd learned, it was to pick her battles. "Okay. Well, I'll put a granola bar in this pocket in case you get hungry, okay?"

With Trey finally ready to go, she trotted over to the end table where her own oversized bag was packed for every imaginable contingency, including a small umbrella. She'd intended to lay it by the door last night but fell asleep immediately when her bed beckoned to her. Getting Trey into his PJs while half asleep and of little help was all she could manage. She hadn't made it back into the living room. Just washed up and went to bed.

They managed to get out of the house and into her car only a few minutes late. But she always had a built-in cushion. When they passed under the Galloway Sons Farm sign, the dash clock read ten minutes before 8 o'clock.

Bree inhaled a breath. If Gage was a Galloway son, that made Trey a Galloway grandson. What did his future hold?

"A cow." Trey pointed out the window.

"Sure is. That's what I tried to tell you. You're going to see the real thing today."

"I'm not a baby. I've seen farm animals."

No point in telling him this time was different. These cows might be his inheritance one day.

They finally pulled in toward the main buildings, and she

tried to decide whether to go toward the smaller one, not that it would ever be considered small. Her entire apartment would likely fit in one of the rooms.

Gage stepped out onto the porch, his cowboy hat in hand. His hair had more wave to it, and she wondered if he'd just stepped out of the shower. Butterflies tumbled in her stomach.

He placed his hat on his head and walked to Trey's side of the vehicle. "Good morning, Trey. I've been waiting for you. We've got lots to do today."

"I'm ready." Trey unlatched his seatbelt. Gage opened the door, and the boy hopped out, feet landing solidly on the ground.

Gage's smile at Trey melted Bree's heart. "Thought we might start with breakfast."

"I'm starving." He had the courtesy to at least look at his mom and shrug.

"I've got bacon, pancakes, fruit, and whatever Cecilia's cooked up."

Bree thought her stomach rumbled at hearing the list. Or maybe she'd imagined that. "You're making my smoothie look pathetic in comparison."

"There's plenty. Come join us."

The Dale Murphy Festival breathing down her neck didn't leave her any wiggle room for fun. "What a sweet offer, but I can't. Not today."

He gave her a look that was unreadable. Disappointment? Relief? "Oh right. Point is for you to get a lot done. Well, don't let us keep you."

Trey threw his body weight against the car door and it clunked shut. "Bye, Mom." The man and boy turned to go.

Bree's eye caught something in the back seat. "Hey, you forgot your bag. The toys. Your snack."

Trey took Gage's hand. "Don't need it."

As she drove down the drive, she watched them in the rear-view mirror until they were out of sight.

Pulling into the edge of town, the sights took her back to childhood. Fair rides were parked in the grassy field by the utility office, their parts that would swing people high in the air or whirl them around folded down or disengaged. Old cars, their paint polished to the perfect shine were parked in several driveways, brought out from their storage sheds for the special occasion. She pulled over to the side of the street, got out her poster, and carried it with a hammer and tiny nail. She pounded the nail and hung the sign directing people to the museum on a utility pole. People complained about the signs, but visitors to town read them, and maybe this house with a banner with the movie star's image and name on it wouldn't turn her in. The U.S. flags hanging down from the light poles lining the streets brought it all together.

A few minutes later, she pulled up to the museum. The sun glinted off its roof, and she knew the weekend would be good, no matter the outcome in her cashier's drawer. Some things were more important than money. Love of commumity. The legacy of those who had come before.

She pulled open the door and inhaled the aroma of the new

material. Since she was a little girl, she'd known that smell as well as her mother's perfume. She ran her fingers across the row of shirts, admiring the various colors and bold design again. Her grandma had said the seller needed to love the merchandise as much as the customer, and Bree most certainly did. She reached out her hand and felt the softness, stopping short of rubbing it next to her cheek, in case a dash of her makeup might mar the newness. When the weekend was over, she'd get her chance and keep one for her own personal collection.

A glimpse of the postman coming up the porch steps awakened her from her memories. She opened the door, and he caught himself from setting it in the wicker love seat on the porch, handing it to her instead. "Happy Dale Murphy weekend," he said, full of cheer, and climbed back into his little vehicle.

She called out, "You have a good one, too!"

This was the part she liked. The sleepy little town came alive during this event. Yards were spruced up. People called in family and threw stew in the crockpot—or left the cooking equipment in the cabinet and trekked the streets for vendors that sold corn dogs and tenderloins, lemon shake-ups and elephant ears. The eating plan thrown aside for a day or three. She couldn't call Mom, and a familiar ache played in her chest. Her memories were all around her, literally. Jo was special to her and would need to be enough. She'd show Trey what his family had done to sustain the town.

*Lord, give us a little family of our own, in your timing.*

She shoved aside the thoughts and pulled out the paperwork.

Her least favorite, taking inventory, still had to be done. The accountant needed to be appeased, even if she'd become a friend as they'd pored over the books, trying to squeak out every last penny so she wouldn't go under. Counting inventory was part of tracking cash flow.

A random stranger would come in every once in a while, and she welcomed the interruption. But she kept to her task. It was now or never because soon she'd be swamped and her chance to keep the books would dissipate.

Before she knew it, the bell overhead jangled, and she placed her best smile for customers on her face. In walked Gage and Trey. Her heart softened at the tall man in a cowboy hat, a relaxed grin on his face, and her son. Their son. Not only did the colors of their features match, but their physiques and grace in the way they carried themselves verified undeniably they were father and son. Bree's heart skipped a beat, happy to see them interacting.

"Hey, I thought I was supposed to come pick Trey up?"

"Oh, I couldn't resist seeing you in your element. Anyway, with my helper, I got my chores done early." He beamed at Trey.

She doubted that was the case. Whenever Trey was around, her tasks took much longer, although she wouldn't trade the companionship for efficiency.

"I played with Bentley, his dog! I brushed a horse, Mommy."

Could her heart melt any more than it was right now? "Oh, wonderful, just like you've always wanted to?"

"Dad let me ride 'im."

"When you've got a boy as talented as Trey is around

animals, he needs to ride, make up for lost time. I stayed with him, should've asked ahead. Hope it's okay." Gage looked more pleased than Trey, if that were possible.

"Parents go with their gut, and I'm glad you did."

His cheeks might be showing a blush, although she'd never seen that before and couldn't be sure. "Seemed like the thing to do. How're the festival duties going, darling?" He glanced at her paperwork on the counter, her pen where she'd tossed it.

"Great. Thanks for asking."

"I might not understand your enthusiasm but you're contagious. Almost makes me a history fan."

That was a start, and she'd take it.

Trey wasn't one to stand around and chat. "I want a shirt."

"Can you rephrase that, using a special word?"

"May I please have a shirt?"

Gage watched them. Maybe he'd carry her efforts forward?

"Yes, you may." She went over to the short clothes rack with kids' sizes.

Traditionally, every year, he was the only one who got a shirt before she saw what sold. "What color? You know you're my best advertisement."

Gage and Trey came and stood beside her. Gage's woodsy, clean scent wafted over as he helped Trey wriggle out of his shirt and into one he'd picked out. Even mixed in with some horse and work odors, her heart fluttered.

She needed to get a grip. Gage would only ever be her son's

father. The sooner she accepted that, the easier life would be. Now if she could only get her hormones to cooperate.

# Chapter 12

Gage headed to the museum first thing in the morning and opened the museum door minutes after Bree unlocked the place for the public.

"What are you doing here?"

She would know if he made something up, so he kept it simple and told her the truth. "I'm here for you. This week it sounds like your hours are brutal."

Her fingers that were clenched by her side loosened. "I have to believe you know something about a demanding job. Things aren't that different in any field, are they? I appreciate your coming."

"Thought maybe you could even use some help, darling."

She gave him the look she'd given him when they were in school, and rolled her eyes. "Right. Just like sophomore year when you volunteered to help in concessions and ate as much as you sold."

He couldn't put anything past her. He liked that. "Well, Kristin told me she called off of some things she promised. Guess I'm her replacement."

This was as good a time as any to show his tools. Gage yanked at his back jeans pocket. "Brought my own dust cloth, really a handkerchief, as Dad used to call them. Where do I start?"

She gave an exaggerated sigh. "Just like in school, I'm not in a position to turn down any assistance. And maybe give me that vintage bandana. Maybe I'll put it on display in the local history area."

"Do you see *everything* as history?"

"Yeah. Yes, I do. Pieces of the past are all around us, and we can learn a lot from them. The more people see that, the better off they'll be."

"Okay. We don't have to agree on everything."

Her shoulders slumped, and he hated he'd let her down. "You can start at the mantle. I'll go grab some furniture polish and cleaning materials."

He couldn't bring himself to stuff his hankie back in his pocket. Gage folded the cloth into a square and placed it on the desk. Ugh. Now she had him thinking like she did.

She returned and went to the fireplace. "Here's Dale's family Bible. Mine too, really. It means a lot to me as a reminder of what a movie star and a small-town girl had in common. You wouldn't touch it with any of these cleaning chemicals. Maybe start by moving everything off and over to the desk." She paused. "This doesn't seem right, your helping."

"Don't over think it. We've been through a lot together." He moved toward the mantel and removed an award Dale had won for her horse-riding skills, and a bobble head of her. He considered what to say and how much. "You've done an awful lot for Trey, and I guess it's just hitting me. Yesterday he asked me questions the entire time about what horses eat. What they like to do. How they have babies."

"Oh, those are all good ones, especially that last one." She seemed overly occupied with moving a Dale Murphy movie in its case back to where it belonged. "I hope he didn't slow you down getting your work done too much."

"That's not what I'm saying. You know yourself that answering him takes time. We might have taken longer with the chores. I'm sure we probably did. But he's got such a sharp mind and absorbed what I was saying like a sponge. The time flew by. It was an amazing morning, and you've raised him so well."

She finished spreading out jewelry, bookmarks, and playing cards of Grace in the display case and straightened up to look at him. "Thanks, but he's partly just like that by nature. He's both of us. It's like God took two opposite people and put the best parts of them in our child."

"I wish you'd take credit for what you've done. I used to think maybe I was confident enough for both of us. But I was wrong."

"If it makes you feel any better, his teacher pulled me aside and said to me, 'You need to talk to him more.' She laughed when she said it, so I knew she was teasing. She explained how he's so engaged with everything in class, she can tell he's had a lot of individual attention."

"See, even a professional educator noticed."

The sun shone through the front window just right, and she'd never looked so radiant. As he noticed her hair and the grace with which she handled a small pocket mirror with a Grace logo, something shifted. A strange sensation he'd never felt before, of affection and admiration and maybe something else.

"I did thank her, I'll have you know. Accepted her compliment wholeheartedly."

A strand of her hair fell over her face, and he was close enough that he tucked it back behind her ear before he could stop himself. Maybe held on a bit, appreciating its soft, silky feel on his fingers. "Guess there's still hope for you yet."

Something in the air crackled between them. "Belief is such a positive force. When I was struggling to keep Trey alive, and that's no exaggeration, I used to think of you. To try to gain strength and play movies in my mind with you meeting him one day, to keep me going."

"My learning about Trey so very late hurt both of us. It's hard to remember that sometimes. I missed everything, but you didn't have the support." It seemed the most natural thing in the world when he brushed his hand over her fingers that rested on the counter. They were warm and soft, and he pulled away before he got too attached.

The bell over the door jangled. She put distance between

them and called in a somewhat breathy tone, "Welcome to the Murphy Museum," as a man and woman he'd never seen before stepped into the foyer.

Once Bree had shown them which rooms had what artifacts, the couple wandered around on their own. "I let them explore on their own but am here if they need me," she said.

Gage tried to stay out of her way. But he couldn't take the silence and wanted to engage her. He wished they could have a relationship without all the heavy stuff between them.

He was dusting some photos in a private room and found one to show her. "I've been wondering about something."

When she noticed he had a vintage photo, she perked up. "Really, what have you got there? I love old photos. But then, anything old appeals to me."

"I think you're getting to me. Here's a photo of somebody that looks a lot like me—two somebodies, actually—and like Trey too. Too bad there aren't names on the back."

Bree took the photo, being careful to keep her fingers off of the image. "About 50% of our photos don't have names. I'm sorry. Sometimes, volunteers come in and match them up with a list we have going."

"Well, I rely on intuition a lot in my work. I feel this might be important and would like to run it through a forensic guy I know."

"Sure, I can scan a copy for you. But would you mind if I look into it first? There are lots of techniques to try. There's so much in here, Gage. Wouldn't it be neat if this had significance for your family? For Trey's family?"

She winced, a pained expression coming over her. "Honestly, it's not going to be easy for me to share him. I'm really glad you're in Trey's life, though. I've had years of him all to myself. I just don't know how I'll manage to be away from him for days on end. We can't avoid the lawyers forever. We'll have to put guidelines in place, if only to protect him."

She wandered off, and looked a bit lost, which was unusual for her.

He wanted to go and put his arms around her but wasn't sure if that would really help. So when the noon siren rang, he knew it was time to go. "Hey, I'm going to grab some lunch and go get Trey from the babysitters like we agreed."

She nodded.

Why did he want to fix things for Bree? Because he'd always gotten along well with her, and she had a heart of gold. They'd always known they could rely on one another, which meant a lot to a kid like him who had it all yet had doubts and desires different from his family.

He wished he could keep her in his life but adult men and women didn't have friends like that, did they?

She'd want more than he could give, going all over the world the way he did. Wouldn't she?

# Chapter 13

"I thought you were on track to get this done at a normal hour," Kristin said, examining Bree as she leaned over the papers full of numbers that were spread out over the museum's counters.

"I know." Bree looked up from the papers. "Having Gage helping earlier was a good thing, to an extent. But he was also a total distraction. I can't thank you enough for coming in this evening."

"It's enjoyable. Extras showed up in the volunteer squad for Keith, Sarah, and Bailey. It's the most exciting time for Fair Creek. You know that. Ever since we rode the church float when we were in the fourth grade, I've been hooked."

"I know what you mean. I don't know why I'm getting so worked up this year, other than I'm afraid I'm going to have to close the museum if we don't have a good turnout. Well, that's a good reason.

"That would stress anyone out. Maybe you would feel better if you had a Plan B."

"Like what? My family tried everything over the years. Tried having two festivals one year, one on Dale's birthday and one like this one, the last weekend closest to her date of death. You haven't forgotten how we combined a special event with the high school homecoming when out-of-towners might be in have you?"

Kristin's eyes spit fire at the suggestion. "Hardly. I was one of the ones who came back, and I hated high school and never cared about homecoming. Whenever anything was planned, I showed up. Sometimes, it's easy to get so immersed in what you're into that you don't see that others are right there with you."

"I hadn't thought of it that way. Didn't mean to offend you."

"You haven't. But these are good memories I don't want to forget myself. You and I weren't close then. This all happened way before Leo came into the picture. My ex and I were going through infertility treatments, and I was having gargantuan mood swings from the meds and my hormones, including that I burst into tears every time I caught a whiff of a baby. But when your mom asked, I agreed to be a judge for the new baby parade they came up with."

Bree took a breath and let it out. "Oh wow, I'd forgotten all about this. I love these old memories."

"Little ones from newborns up to age three dressed up like vintage cowgirls and cowboys of the Dale Murphy era.

Your genius mom found costumes online and sold them for a reasonable price, for a fundraiser. The day came, and I sat with a tissue box and wept through it, lied and told the other judges I had allergies, cried my way along. I've loved it all. Wouldn't trade any of it. Point being, I've been all in for whatever this museum, really your family, had going. So have most of the people in this little town."

Kristin picked up another paper and looked at inventory, checking boxes as she talked. "This shouldn't take too long."

"How do you work on two things at once, Kristin? And do a rant too?"

"Wow, I needed you here earlier. Too bad it didn't work out."

"I have a feeling even my multi-tasking skills wouldn't have saved the day with Gage Galloway in the room. What charisma, and I know he's got even more effect on you."

Bree rolled her eyes and directed her focus on her work. That last remark didn't even deserve a response. "I'd like to hear more about this Plan B. Whenever I get too tight a grip on what I want to happen, it doesn't work out." That counted double for whatever she wanted from Gage.

Kristin put down her paper. "I always do better when I let go and let God. You're not in control of anything, certainly not the weather. Hey, there's always starting an online account to raise money as an option. You know, when someone announces they're going to have to close their business because of lack of sales, or their building needs renovated or whatever? People chip in whatever they can and, if you get enough people, it all adds up."

Bree couldn't believe what she was hearing. She put her hands on her hips for emphasis. "I'd never do that. Ask for a handout? As important as this is to keep going, I can't damage the family name. Murphys stand on their own two feet. I've just got to offer an experience people want to come to and spend their money on."

"Whoa. That's old school thinking. Watch out for getting so caught up in history you don't pay attention to history in the making. Crowd funding is totally legit. Think of it like a barn raising in the old days. Don't get stagnant in the here and now or you'll lose people. It's challenging, staying current and preserving the past at the same time. People don't respect history like they used to. It isn't your fault, not all in your hands to change it."

Bree didn't know what to think. So she went over to Kristin and gave her a bear hug. "Thanks for straightening me out and making me feel I'm not alone."

Kristin swept the back of her hand over her own forehead, as if she were wiping off sweat. "Whew! That's what friends are for. Didn't mean to go off on you like that."

"Glad you did. The end is in sight so let's finish up. Gage will be picking up Trey soon and bringing him here. We're going to ride around town and check out how this festival is coming to life, like a sleepy giant. Trey and I love this part every year."

Once her friend had left, Bree tackled her work with new zeal and purpose. Whenever her energy flagged, Kristin's pep talk fueled her. She could only do her part, and if the museum meant enough to enough people, it would go on.

The bell on the door jingled and Bree glanced at the clock on the wall with Dale Murphy's image as its face. Nearly two hours had slipped by. Kristin had left and returned home earlier.

Trey burst in, coming at her at a gallop. "Mommy, I rode in Daddy's truck." He wrapped his arms around her.

She patted his shoulder and gave him a squeeze. "That sounds amazing."

Gage hesitated before entering, as though he was letting them have their moment. Or maybe their exchange earlier still stung? Then he walked into the center of the room, and her breath caught. He smiled, and that along with his relaxed stance, all six foot three of him, made her want to hug him too. Maybe plant a kiss even.

What was wrong with her? He was her kid's dad. Maybe chatting about hormones with Kristin had put hers into overdrive.

She loosened Trey's grip on her, took his hand, and led him over to Gage together. "Monster hug." It was a code they used when they felt extra warmly about someone, usually a family member, and wanted to show them. She and Trey formed a tiny circle around Gage, gave him a quick hug, then stood back.

Gage's eyebrow quirked up. "What's this about?"

"We think you're pretty special for fitting us in, with everything you have to do with your own work. Some people wouldn't have come back after what I said to you."

Gage's face might have shown a little redness, and she hadn't meant to make him uncomfortable. "Enough with the mushiness. Let's do that drive around town like you promised."

Trey grabbed her hand. "Yes. I want to. Come on, Mommy."

# Chapter 14

Gage opened the door for Trey and Bree, and they stepped out onto the museum's porch. Trey slipped his hand into his, and how small it was next to his brought him into another space. What kind of world would he grow up in? How could they best prepare him for all that he might encounter? He had no idea, and none of these hard questions had been on his radar until meeting his son.

He and Trey arrived at the truck, and then he looked back to where Bree still stood on the porch. She rested her hip on the railing and removed her cell phone from holding it up to her eye.

"Look at this sky. It's like God's art every day. I've never seen such little bundles of clouds tucked into pretty strips of golds and pinks, have you?"

Trey ran back to Bree. "Take a selfie of me, Mommy, please?"

"Okay, let's stand over there, sweetie. The angle will be better."

"I don't look around me that much like you do. Maybe I should start. I've spent most of my time in cities or in places where I can't afford the time to be a stargazer. What's happening on the ground has to be paid attention to."

But he wasn't sure if he could make that kind of change or if he wanted to. Being around Trey, with his endless questions.

"Come here," Trey said. "I want our family in it."

A family. Gage hadn't thought of the three of them that way and wasn't sure if he wanted to. He didn't move. This little trip around town would take forever if they dawdled along, and they weren't away from the museum yet. Maybe if he waited and didn't run up there, they'd move along.

"Come on, Daddy."

Bree had the courtesy to look like she knew Trey was asking a lot. "Hey, not everybody's into selfies. You don't have to if you don't want to, Gage."

She shifted slightly from where Trey stood. "We can get one of the three of us later." Trey's smile faded and he shuffled his feet a little in the direction Bree wanted him to go.

This was such a small request, and Gage was making it a big deal. "Wait, I'll come over and we'll get the best selfie ever."

Trey's smile was all the reward he needed. "Yay."

Bree beamed. "Now get in between the grown-ups. Let's kneel."

She held the camera up high, snapped photos, then let Trey view them and weigh in. "Can you make me taller?"

He picked Trey up and held him facing out for a photo. "Give it time, buddy. One day, you'll be tall as me."

The admiration in Trey's eyes toward his dad made a special moment. Bree snapped a photo of the two of them, blinking quickly so she could see to focus the phone just so.

Finally, they were done, and Trey approved the final result. "You're a hard riding cowboy, you know that? This one really is adorable. Mind if I post it online?"

Yes, Gage really didn't want the social media intrusion. Everything seemed like new territory all of a sudden. He wasn't a fan of social media. You never knew what strangers might be watching. He'd seen it in his work. But maybe this was one area he needed to compromise on.

"Sure, go ahead." He managed to sound light-hearted. Maybe people really could change. There wasn't a better reason for making adjustments than having a kid in his life now.

After Bree hit send, Gage made himself stay until she was ready to leave. She liked moving slow, and he needed to give her that. He let her lead them away, but couldn't help calling out, "Let me get the door for you."

She turned to look back. "Oh, we're not driving. I thought we'd walk to go get our golf cart."

Trey jumped up and down. "Yesss! Golf carts."

Pint-sized fingers connected with Gage's, and he gave a little squeeze this time. When Bree took her position on the other side, Trey held her hand too.

Gage couldn't stifle a grin. It had been a great day hanging out with his son. But having Bree in the mix made it three times better. "Lead the way."

She started them off walking along the sidewalk, which was barely wide enough for them to walk side-by-side. "The golf carts are on Jefferson. It's a side street. We better hurry. They close soon."

He picked up his pace but couldn't do too much or he'd leave Trey behind. "Nobody's going to rush me," he teased. He picked his feet up higher and marched.

"Me either." Trey started running, pulling both adults along. The storefronts of the little shops went by. A few had brochures taped to their windows that showed what times various festival events were.

After struggling to hold Trey back, Bree said, "I'll let you go ahead of us these several yards, if you're careful. The golf carts are up ahead from here. Go on ahead. We'll catch up."

Hit the Nail hardware's windows were custom painted with a bright-orange pumpkin patch. The thrift store for the town's charity held a Dale Murphy-inspired white cowboy hat on a mannequin dressed in her signature Western-styled fringed skirt and matching top.

This whole thing, with holding hands and planning to ride around in a golf cart, was what his friends in news would have called "cheesy." Here he was totally on board for it. Later, he might analyze why this really did feel important, even compelling, like Bree had said everyday life could be. Everybody liked cheese, so maybe the word had been given a bad name. Being together and making life better for a child mattered. Having a hand in his felt right. He was at a loss to know what could matter more.

Bree quietly said to Gage over Trey's head, "Notice there are a few people walking around? There are always some that come in early. It's begun. Isn't it exciting?" Slightly out of breath, her words came out in puffs. He wasn't sure if their quick walking caused that or what. Her enthusiasm was contagious though. Somehow, he wanted her to succeed more than he'd thought possible.

"If you say so." They passed a man with a camera strap around his neck who stood taking a photo of a building. "What is somebody in their thirties doing? I mean you grew up with her but . . ." He didn't want to burst her bubble, but thinking everyone was into Dale shouldn't be supported.

"You really have to ask? Dale's a legend, and new people of every age find her movies all the time. The fan club's tiny but devoted. They call themselves Murphites."

He led the three of them around a place where the sidewalk had bubbled up from a huge tree root. "What?"

"Rhymes with Vegemite. A couple from Australia wanted the nickname to reflect their favorite sandwich spread down under. The group took a vote and their idea won."

He swung his arm a little, bringing Trey's with him. "Doing okay, buddy? Well, darling, you're once again proving that truth really is stranger than fiction. Maybe corn's one of the main ingredients in Vegemite?"

"I don't interfere with anything the fans want. They're sweethearts and they're quirky and fun. I'm glad Dale has fans after all these years. Wish there were more. Anyway, the bank he photographed has kept the original structure. It was built in 1880. Dale Murphy's epic photo in front of it made it famous. You remember the one?"

Not exactly. Having the guts to tell her that when she talked so obsessively about history took a lot. "What if I said no, darling?"

Coming up to the little green sign that said Jefferson, they turned and the grassy lot full of golf carts came into view. Trey pulled them harder.

"Not going to lie, I'd be super disappointed." She made a sad face with downturned lips. "On the bright side, there's still time to reform."

"If I only wanted to. The flesh is weak."

"I'm not above staging an intervention. The first step in evolving is seeing the error of your ways."

"I'm open to working with you on this, at least."

They reached the little booth. Someone had scrawled on poster board, "Desiner models cost extra." Ouch, where was the "G?" He had to overlook the spelling mistake, which was hard for someone attuned to words.

Trey came over from where he stood looking at a golf cart, distracting him from his distress. "I want that one."

His boy pointed to a golf buggy that had a lot color to it, and was sportier but Bree didn't take time to reconsider. "Well, we just got a basic one, honey."

Trey's little shoulders slumped. Gage wasn't having it.

For once, maybe he could make a difference. Might be an

actual positive influence on his own kid. He tossed a look over at Bree and spread his palm over his chest and patted twice, indicating he'd handle this. "Maybe it's a guy thing. But I can't take my eyes off that golf buggy myself." He placed his hand lightly on Trey's shoulder. "Will you show me what you like about it?"

Trey nodded, his eyes sparkling like stars.

Bree's mouth formed a straight line, and she stayed put as Trey led Gage back to his favorite. She'd always been stubborn, now that he thought of it. Maybe bull-headed was a better term.

What if he pushed her too far and lost her friendship? They'd be strangers parenting their son. Something inside him ached. He couldn't let that happen.

They reached the specimen of Trey's admiration. Trey circled it on all sides. "See. It's really cool!" A deep blue, the cart's canopy top had mini Colts pennants pointed down all around, like fringe. A large horseshoe, matching the football team's logo, covered the hood of the little vehicle.

"I'm not going to argue with you." The boy nodded as if his head might fly off. "You've got a good eye, Trey. Some people wouldn't appreciate how neat this one is." Gage glanced over where Bree stood with her arms crossed. She pointed to the cell phone in her hand, indicating the time, he supposed.

Trey's head turned to see where Gage was looking. "Mommy's mad."

This was new territory. Gage didn't want to infringe on what seemed like a solid mother/son relationship. Although, how could he really know, not living with Trey 24/7? "Sometimes, adults don't agree. Let's go back and negotiate with your mommy."

Gage walked back toward Bree. Trey skipped along beside him. Gage didn't want to spoil the kid. But as dreams went, a fancy golf cart was relatively modest. Why not go for it? By the time they met up to Bree, Gage had pulled out his wallet from his back pocket. "Trey's picked out the best one for the Galloway men. How about I chip in for an upgrade to the snazzy one?"

Bree's arms were crossed in front of her like a shield of armor. Gage swallowed, He didn't like this, being out of her good graces.

"What'll it be, folks? I'm closing up shop." The lot manager joined the discussion.

"Can we get it, Mommy?"

Bree's hands fell to her side. "I ordered this early, prepaid, and got the best rate."

The lot manager swiped his hands on a cloth he'd been using to wipe down his merchandise. "The boss always lets me bring extra models. Sometimes, customers will fall in love. Paperwork's no problem. Cover the upcharge and she's yours."

Bree gave the slightest nod.

There was no time to waste. Gage handed over his credit card. "Put the extra on that."

When the paperwork was filled out, which involved more signatures than when he'd signed liability waivers to risk his life going overseas, they were done.

Bree slid into the driver's seat. "Get in beside me, Trey." The boy didn't have to be asked twice and hopped in.

Gage slid onto the back seat. She'd agreed to his wishes, and he wasn't going to let on how much he wanted to feel that steering wheel in his hands and whirl around town. "Hold on tight there, partner."

Bree nodded. "Safety first. That's why I'm driving. Never know what a guy new to golf carts might do on the open streets."

"Yeah, it goes all of thirty miles an hour at top speed."

Trey bounced on the seat. "Wow." At least he was unaware of their tension.

After making sure Trey was focused on his surroundings and holding on, Bree caught Gage's eye and gave him a steely look. He surprised himself that he could read her lips while no sound came out. "We need to talk."

"Sure, darling, something to look forward to." Oh good, he couldn't wait.

Their first squabble as parents. Might as well get started. There were many more in their future, from what he'd heard. Truth of the matter was, he'd always found Bree entertaining when she got fired up about something. Even if it was his behavior.

# Chapter 15

Bree stood at the foot of Trey's bed and smiled down at his angelic face as he slept. She hadn't planned for the ride in the golf cart to last so long. Standing next to her, Gage's plaid flannel shirtsleeves were rolled up. Even his forearms were ripped. Something stirred in her that she hadn't felt in a long time, if ever. His aftershave wafted over, and she discreetly inhaled. When he lifted his arm as though it might land on her shoulder, her heart rate skipped up a notch. Then he casually touched his cowboy hat instead. With effort, she held in a moan.

Spending more time with him proved challenging, in more ways than one. They had major differences in their personalities, yet sometimes they were perfectly in tune, like now.

Trey's eyes had fallen to half-mast immediately when they coaxed him into lying down, and then his eyes closed altogether.

She pointed toward their son's bedroom door, leading the way out as Gage followed.

Once they'd reached her living room, Bree figured it was safe to talk without Trey waking up, let alone hearing and comprehending their conversation.

"I'm craving a warm drink. Would you like some cocoa or tea? I'll hand it to you, Gage. You make it awfully hard to stay mad at you." She swatted his shoulder, making contact with solid muscle. When would she learn? Touching him had the opposite effect of lightening the mood, like she'd aimed for. They were alone, and it seemed warm in here. "I mean, who knew you're funnier than a six-year-old, or at least can entertain one with jokes all night?"

He grinned and seemed to let out a breath. "Could be a TV show there." She had said she'd wanted to talk and meant to start with a compliment, then get to the rough stuff. At the golf cart place, he'd disrespected her opinion. But maybe he did care what she thought, and finding common ground was a better way to start.

"Cocoa would hit the spot." He quirked an eyebrow, and his brown eyes sparkled. "Maturity isn't one of my strengths. Glad that's not a bad thing." He was irresistible when he was full of mischief, always had been. She was in so much trouble.

She swallowed and nearly sprinted for the kitchen and some breathing room. Gage followed right along. *Breathe, Bree.* "I know I called this meeting. But I've had a change of heart, honestly. My funds are tight, and I thought the Colts golf cart was frivolous.

But somehow it doesn't seem like that big a deal now. Thanks for helping pay for it."

"I didn't think he'd become a juvenile delinquent by getting what he wanted. If I'm proved wrong, I'll pay the legal fees to clear his record."

She giggled and reached into the cabinet for the mugs and cocoa powder. "I've always been a serious person. Becoming a mom might have sent me over the top that way, at times."

He ran his fingers through his hair. "Ya think so, maybe just a little?"

Her eyes locked onto those long fingers in his thick, wavy tresses, and she wondered what the texture would feel like between her own fingers.

*Focus, Bree.*

"I wanted him to have his dad, for all the normal reasons. My dad was pretty absent, if you remember. But I hadn't realized how nice it would be to have a hand with making the everyday decisions." Except it wasn't nice at all earlier. But she could see he was trying and didn't want to hurt him. She finished making their drinks and handed him his mug.

He took a drink. "Thanks, it's good. My way of looking at things—my humor, if you will—has gotten me into trouble my whole life. I used to try to change. But I really couldn't. It's nice to think I might be appreciated, as a dad."

"Well, you're way too muscular to have a 'dad bod.' So falling back on jokes isn't the worst way to get into the Dad Club."

*Why was she talking about his body, of all subjects?*

"I think we both know I never intended to get into what you call the Dad Club, darling. It was partly because I didn't have the great childhood everybody thought."

"Really. I thought we knew one another, but there are always depths to people that are unknown. You seemed easy going and well liked at school."

They both sipped their drinks for a bit in silence. She went over to the couch and sunk in among the cushions. He chose the other end and did the same.

A few seconds passed, and he situated himself on the cushion facing her. "Part of why I had to get away, even with a good family, is how I was treated in school. The guidance counselor, who knew all about careers, shoved me into the vocational track. Didn't you find it odd I was gone from school most of the day senior year? Nothing wrong with the trades. I wanted something different though."

She put her mug down and wrinkled her brow. "How come you never told me this?"

He took a sip, and it was as if she could see the warm liquid flow, working its magic, before he answered. "It's the most important things, the most painful, that you never tell anyone. Right? Maybe remember that about Trey as he grows."

For someone who hadn't chosen to be a father, he had wisdom about kids that made her stop and think. He'd gotten more attuned to himself while they were apart. "All the kids knew you could do anything, that your jokes meant you were smart and saw life deeply. Humor isn't easy to pull off."

"That's why I kept what the counselor said to myself, darling. I didn't want you to prop me up. It's the administrators that make the difference, that get the references together. I didn't need the scholarships. Everybody knew that too. When I was a little older than Trey, the kids made fun of me for my nice clothes, my high-quality leather boots—basically for whatever they didn't have. Galloways weren't hurting for money. But that didn't mean we didn't hurt."

She rested her hand on his arm, then liked the feeling so much she removed it. "Even if I couldn't help, I wish I'd known."

He shrugged. "I survived. The experience made me the tough guy I am today." He gave her that look between a smirk and a grin. It was impossible to fight off his brand of adorable. For her anyway.

"You've got me spilling my guts. What's with you and the museum? I don't get it. But I'm willing to try."

Her adrenaline flowed as if she were in danger, and maybe she was. "Let me get you some more to drink first."

She'd made extra, so she put all of it into a different, huge mug, and placed it into the microwave and warmed it up, then headed back. She put the mug on the table and went the few steps to look out the window into the dark night. "How can you not see it's about the museum, that Dale Murphy has fans around the world that need her? Her movies still touch people."

He picked up the mug, faked he was going to drop it. "Is this the biggest mug you have? I mean, I could sip this puppy all the way across Galloway Sons Farm and back."

Bree smiled. She'd always loved a challenge. Educating others was part of her job. "Dale worked to get where she was, took the bit parts, believed in herself, even though she came from this tiny town. And women got no respect then. She's my blood relative."

He set the mug down, got up, and went where she stood and stared into her eyes. "If you're passionate about her, that goes a long way with me."

"You're sweet. So many people think everything's temporary. They want to tear down the buildings. If no one comes here and shows interest, that's what they'll do. That little triangle building where my mom took me to get doughnuts before I started school, they want to tear that down."

A wrinkle appeared on his forehead. "There's nothing like that one anywhere I've ever been, darling. I have memories. That one would hurt."

"The fountains and trees, the school buildings where drama students acted, track athletes ran on. Next thing it'll be people, the ones who care about memories and have the most years stored up inside them."

He took another drink. "You sure that cocoa you drank wasn't spiked?"

She laughed, and her jaw relaxed. Maybe his humor served a purpose, especially for her. "We better wrap this up. But Dale Murphy's my dad's cousin. He wasn't around for me, but she was a part of him, and a part of my DNA. Without standing on the shoulders of our relatives, what future can we hope to have?"

He lifted his mug and stood, and then shook his head, as if

clearing off the heavy mood for them both. "I can't drink all this. I'd sink into a sugar coma. Hey, Wyatt and Kristin invited us over to the house for supper tomorrow. They want to meet Trey. Get him together with Max. I know the timing's not great."

She gave him credit that he seemed to know when to lighten things up, a talent she admired and hadn't been blessed with. "That's really nice of them. I just… You know I'm slammed." She headed into the kitchen and toward the door to the outside.

"What? You're resisting the Galloway Sons Invitational? You might be surprised to hear this coming from me, but family's everything. Kid needs his mommy there for this. You gotta eat. We won't keep you, and he can stay longer."

She ran water from the faucet into a glass and took a swallow. "Of course, I'll come. You welcoming him is the best. I'm grateful."

"Well, if you need some space, here's something to look forward to. I'll be going to DC for a high-level meeting the day after the festival."

Her heart hurt for some reason. "That's not what I meant, that I wanted you to leave. You know how important the festival is to me. And Trey lives for his time he spends with you every day."

He sighed. "I tried every way, including setting up online meetings, but it's involved. It's going to last a few days. Like you said, so eloquently, there's nothing like being there in person."

How would they manage when he went back to work for good? She wouldn't be one of those moms who shipped her kid off on a plane for the weekend.

Gage didn't say much, seeming more subdued. She wished she had been more enthusiastic. Maybe he was let down by her hesitation. But hopefully, she'd gotten through to him about her work.

"I'm set up in DC pretty well, with a lot of space. And I get sent out on assignments unexpectedly. You could absolutely come with Trey on his visits. I want you to be comfortable and for him to be safe."

She didn't want to have a long-distance dad relationship for Trey. "I'll think about it." She hadn't tried to sound interested. Gage said goodbye and slipped out the door.

She locked up and sank into bed with her clothes on. If she could only get through meeting all the Galloways, things would be easier.

They were a bunch of cowboys. What could go wrong?

# Chapter 16

It was early to take Trey to the babysitter, but she'd knocked off her to-do list for leaving the house. Bree drove along the road to take Trey to the babysitter and mentally kicked herself about how last night had gone. She'd intended to read Gage the riot act, as her mom used to say but he'd been so darn cute with Trey. She'd just focus on getting to the Galloways tonight and move forward. She normally loved talking to her son in the car on their way to places. But today she'd set up what she called his "happy song" playlist.

His little voice chirped along with the singing. She occasionally glanced in the rearview mirror as he munched on Cracker Jacks and his legs swung back and forth. After Gage had told him about loving the snack, Trey had ditched his goldfish cracker habit and would only eat Cracker Jacks. His favorite song came on, and she looked back in time for him to add in arm motions, practically dancing in his seat.

Maybe it was her imagination, but he seemed happier since meeting his daddy. He'd always been a cheerful, easy-going kid for the most part. Now, his spirits were lifted-up a notch.

"Ee-I-ee-I-oh!" he shouted, full of joy.

Why couldn't she be more optimistic? She hated that she'd exchanged the struggle of worrying her son would never have a dad in his life to concerns about how she'd work out all the details so he could see his dad.

And what was wrong with her? She'd wanted to make a point about how parents should present a united front and not spoil kids. Then she invited him for cocoa, and they'd gotten into a deep discussion. A lot of the hard parts of parenting were still ahead. She didn't want to get too close to Gage. She had too many other priorities to complicate her life like that.

Last night before he left, Gage had offered to keep Trey today. She told him it was best to keep Trey in his routine, especially on the day he would meet Max. Gage had reluctantly agreed, said he had farm work to do.

It would be so much easier to keep her focus if he were an ex and anything romantic was behind them. It sounded like such an awful thing to say, but this dance they were doing was tough. She couldn't let her emotions get in the way of what was best for her son. And she didn't want to get into a romantic relationship, just as she'd never dated, because she didn't want to take her eye off the ball where Trey was concerned. *Your will be done, Lord.*

It sure had been nice to run around with Trey and have another adult to fall back on though.

They arrived at the sitter's house, and she helped Trey from his car seat and walked him to the door. She'd held him back from going into kindergarten until he was more mature and sometimes doubted her decision on that. Going forward, she couldn't imagine having to thrash through every parenting decision with Gage. Fighting over renting a golf cart was the least of her concerns. She'd thought it was about spending the extra money and because she didn't want to spoil Trey. But maybe it had to do with being in control.

Once at work, her morning flew by. She gave instructions to the judges, made sure her inventory was in order for the last time, and went over the assignments Jo had agreed to cover. The people coming to stay in her bedrooms for the bed and breakfast checked in. They'd asked to come ahead so they could enjoy the town before the crowds.

The noon siren sounded, and Jo came in carrying her favorite lunch containers on a tray. The museum had a lot of items, like trays. "Jo, I don't have time for—"

"I know. My ambitions to make comfort food went by the wayside and I stayed up past midnight working on my online shop. Here's some cheese and crackers. Drown yourself in carbs. It's the only way. Give yourself a mental break and let's chat. I've got good news."

"You've talked me into it."

This was the second time someone had to persuade her

to take a break. Did she have a problem? Maybe she'd become too intense, too serious. Oh, brother. Gage had her rethinking everything. It was the last thing she needed, to analyze all of this.

She went over to the desk. Taking a seat, she put together the cheese and crackers and started munching.

Jo carried over a plate of strawberries with the tops still on, arranged with a pile of powdered sugar to dip in. After setting the fruit down, she flopped a newspaper into the center of the table. "Check this out."

A few sentences on the front page teased a story about a museum with Dale Murphy's artifacts and the festival it hosted. Bree's breath caught in her throat. This was a metropolitan newspaper from a few days ago. She took a swig of bottled water that ran down her mouth.

Jo handed her a napkin. "Don't try to hide your excitement."

Bree dabbed her mouth and flipped inside to the story. There wasn't a byline, just said it was written by "staff reports." Things they'd said over the last week were in there. "I've gotta make a call." There was a couple going on a self-guided tour, and she nearly ran them over to get outside and stand on the museum lawn.

After dialing, Gage's deep, familiar voice answered, and Bree didn't hold back. "What did you do?"

"Hope you're not mad, darling. What you said deserved attention. I didn't ask you though, afraid to get your hopes up. Newspapers are bombarded with press releases. Most never see the light of day. You and your event must have held some editor's interest."

"I just…" Her words choked off.

He waited but she didn't recover. "Help me out. Can't tell if you're laughing or crying."

She swallowed and took deep breaths. "Is hysterical an option? Gage, you didn't have to do this. But I'm so glad you did. The weather is in the 75% range to cooperate, but there's a glut of festivals and activities. Publicity's more important than ever."

"Hopefully, that story gives you a chance at increased crowds, anyway. Sorry if I pushed too hard for you to come tonight. I know you've got a lot to do."

"It's okay. You really surprised me. Not just helping with the museum, but wanting me to come with Trey tonight."

"We have history—and I know how much you like that word." Even through the phone, she could tell he was smiling as he continued. "But don't ever assume you know everything about me."

"I won't, not from now on. Thanks, and we'll see you later."

After they ended the call, she worked alone as she bundled up the three bestselling books on Dale Murphy and Fair Creek and put them at a discount for buying together, then tucked them into museum logo bags. She got halfway through creating bundles when her phone alarm went off. In fifteen minutes, she needed to pick up Trey so they could get to dinner on the farm on time. She upped her speed on the bundles, wishing she had more hours in the day to get everything done.

The bell over her front door jingled. An interruption was

going to put her behind, and she'd have to ask the customer to return tomorrow. But she looked up to see Gage enter and walk toward her. He always looked nice, but today his Western-styled shirt in deep brown appeared to be made of expensive material that accentuated his muscles and set off the shade of his eyes. She guessed he'd had his hair cut, and the stubble along his chin wasn't as scruffy. Was his hair around his collar wet from getting out of the shower?

Butterflies fluttered in her stomach. This was just great. She couldn't risk losing Gage's friendship over a little bout of hormones.

When he came closer though, his smile seemed a bit strained, his lips almost a straight line. Could he be nervous? "Your chariot awaits, darling." His deep voice gave nothing away.

"I wasn't expecting you." She picked up the empty logo bags and stacked the books. "You didn't have to come into town to drive me." After bending down and placing everything in a lower cabinet and shutting the door, she stood and faced him. "On the other hand, if you came to gloat over that amazing story you ran for the museum, I'm here for it. Did I mention how awesome you are?"

He took a few steps nearer the counter and then strolled back to where he'd been, two times in a row. "You might have told me…a couple dozen times." He started another round. He was nervous. Her gut clenched. What was he hesitant to tell her?

Gage cleared his throat. "I thought both of us bringing Trey tonight might make him more comfortable. He's young, and he'll look back on this for the rest of his life."

Bree was impressed he'd thought so much about the evening. Gage's joking around sometimes implied he didn't take things seriously. "You're right. He's impressionable. We want to make this as special as we can."

Gage stopped pacing and smiled. His eyes held an extra sparkle. "See, we agree on some things. Giving you a heads-up, he'll be getting some presents. Sort of a welcome to the family party."

A knot formed in Bree's stomach. Maybe meeting the Galloways was a bigger deal than she'd been telling herself. "He loves surprises, and I've tried to teach him to be grateful and have good manners." She grabbed her purse and slung the strap over her shoulder. Arrangements with Trey would not be 100% under her control now, including the presents and party details, and she'd better get used to it.

Gage came closer. "You've done great with him. He's going to be fine. I hope he's thrilled with his party."

"Oh, I'm sure he will be, meeting the rest of his wonderful family." She went over, checked her appearance in the mirror mounted on the wall behind a door, took her lip gloss from her purse and dabbed it on. "Maybe I should have dressed up more for this evening." She could have worn the blouse that flattered her curves instead of this sweatshirt with Dale Murphy splashed all over the front and festival details on the back.

He quirked an eyebrow. "You look great, like a museum mogul. You've really shaped this place up, you know that? I meant every word in that story."

His words washed over her, a balm to her jarred nerves. She really could do this. "Thanks for saying that. You have no idea how much it means. Now, we'd better get Trey to stay on schedule."

He lightly took her elbow as she walked by, guiding her out the door. "You're easy to appreciate, Bree, always have been."

She wouldn't focus on his warm touch.

That was easier said than done as he stood near while she set the security alarm and closed and locked the door. "You know, Gage, spending time with you has made Trey so happy." She started walking to his truck, but the blue of the sky stopped her. He waited, following her gaze, and a whiff of his aftershave made her feel things she hadn't in a long time, if ever. Her words tumbled out. "I used to feel like you and me were complete opposites. Our differences really annoyed me."

"We were like cattle headbutting in the pasture, darling. But at least for tonight, I'm contented as an old cow chewing on her cud. We've had a rough start. But I believe God is showing us the way forward to a bright future, for all of us."

She didn't dare ask what he meant. They reached the truck. He held the door open for her. Bree climbed up on the seat, full of anticipation for Trey's big night. She couldn't help but agree with Gage again. The next couple of hours would be important for her too. She just wasn't quite sure how. But one thing was for sure: she couldn't wait to find out.

Whatever it was, God would touch their lives as he had all along. They just didn't always see how.

# Chapter 17

Gage kept the truck on an even keel as he drove his family to the Galloway Sons Farm dinner. He'd never liked cruise control, not in a vehicle or in life. No matter what his status with Bree, she would always be Trey's mom and part of the Galloway family. He appreciated his options of slowing down or speeding up in everything he did, and when it came to their relationship, even more so.

Bree sat on the truck's long bench seat, far enough away that they weren't near to each other at all. Keeping his eyes on the road was proving difficult. His gaze roamed over so he could look at Bree without her noticing. She sat rigidly, shoulders so tight they were up around her ears. She caught him and faced him with a frown that only upped the tension rolling off her. With her blonde hair loose around her shoulders, the sweatshirt accented her curves and made her simply irresistible.

A low murmuring sound pulled his eyes toward the road, but nothing outside seemed to cause it. He played with the radio's volume, but it wasn't on. Bree noticed and tilted her head toward the back seat, like she was answering the questioning he had.

Their son hummed some children's song Gage couldn't quite identify. Then Trey got to a certain place, and Gage had to resist singing aloud the lyrics that ran through his head. "And Bingo was his Name-O."

They arrived at the farm, and he pulled his truck into a space where someone had tacked a poster with the words "Trey's Dad." "We're here," he said to his passengers, swallowing a lump in his throat. For once, his family had saved the best parking space for him, instead of it being a free-for-all and every man to himself as usual.

Trey bounced in his seat. "We're here, Mommy." Gage exited the vehicle and sprinted around to help Trey disengage from his seat before he took things into his own hands. When Gage popped open the door, Trey said, "Let me do it," and proceeded to get himself out.

"Well, I've never heard you say that before, partner."

Trey rolled his eyes, surprising Gage again with how much humor he could grasp.

Bree seemed to be frozen in place.

He held Trey's hand and guided him to where Gage opened the passenger door for Bree. She smiled, but her lips trembled slightly, unless he'd imagined it. He'd never intended to stress her out, and what if she decided to just send Trey by himself next time?

He gave her his steadiest smile, with no teasing in it. "You've met these people at one time or another."

Trey jumped up and down at his side, pulling his hand. "Let's go, Daddy. I want to meet Max, my cousin."

"He wants to meet you too. Give me a minute until Mommy's ready."

Bree swung her legs around to the side of the seat, positioning herself to climb down. "You're right, of course. I know Sierra from Delaney's, and Kristin and I are close." She glanced down at Trey, as if she didn't want him to hear what she said next.

But Trey only had eyes for his new family that were standing outside in an open area. He was mesmerized by a pile of branches heaped together that had been lit on fire for what looked like an old-fashioned bonfire for a wiener roast.

Gage leaned close to her ear. "I've let my brothers know the situation, and we're all excited, to be honest. It'll be fine. You'll see."

She placed her hand on his arm and slid down the truck seat and out of the truck's cab. "I'm excited too. This just seems different. Let's go get this party started."

The three of them covered the several yards in a couple of minutes or less, and when they were almost there, Wyatt came out to meet them, with Max sitting on his shoulders.

"Pick me up, Daddy." So now Gage had to compete with what other kids got to do? This parenting thing really was relentless.

He eyed Bree, who now had something else to worry about, he presumed, since he had never had a child on his shoulders, and Bree probably knew it. Just as he figured he'd give it a go, Wyatt brought Max down from his shoulders.

Gage encircled Bree with one arm and put his other on Trey's shoulder. "Wyatt, you may remember Bree. This is my son, Trey. Bree's his mommy."

Wyatt dipped his head toward Bree, aiming a smile at her from under his cowboy hat before he put his hand out for Trey to take, and the child shook hands. "It's so nice to meet you, Trey. I hope you like hotdogs and marshmallows melted over the fire." Wyatt's words seemed overly formal, but Trey was wide-eyed and nodded solemnly, like he was taking everything in.

"I love hotdogs!"

Wyatt then dropped down to the level of both boys, and Gage followed his lead. When Wyatt took Trey in a bear hug, Gage was unprepared for what it meant to see his brother hug his son for the first time.

Gage swallowed the lump in his throat. "Trey," Gage said, "this is your cousin, Max."

The boys looked at each other. Little Max hugged Trey just as he'd seen his daddy hug him. The two boys stayed in an embrace for what seemed like minutes but could only have lasted several seconds. For Gage, everything felt like it was in slow motion. After the boys pulled apart, both jiggled and fiddled around, full of pent-up energy they didn't know how to express, as far as Gage could tell.

Breaking away from her position behind the men and boys, Bree strode over and took Trey's hand. "Why don't we go over and see what everyone else is doing?" She held out her other hand and Max grabbed on. "I want to say hi to your mommy, Max, to thank her again for the pretty balloons she made for Trey's party."

After Bree and the boys made their way over toward the wienie roast area, Wyatt hugged Gage. For Gage to have his brother's strength and support, at a time like this, meant everything. As good as Wyatt's gesture felt, the boys had the right idea about keeping it short.

Gage pulled away first. "Good grief, I've never hugged so much in my life."

Wyatt pointed to a big tree that used to drop massive numbers of buckeyes they collected as kids. "We have a tree over there we like to hug, if you're interested."

Seriously? He hadn't been around. But his family had gone soft since their parents had passed, obviously. How should he handle this? Before he generated a comeback, Wyatt spoke. "Come on, I'm kidding."

Gage didn't like how close he'd come to making a fool of himself. "Of course, you are. Look, if you're going to make us roast our own hotdogs, let's get started."

"All right, sorry that I couldn't resist pulling your leg about the tree hugging. But, for real, we have more surprises that'll likely lead to more hugs, but you don't have to become a tree hugger."

Gage didn't know how much more of this he could take.

"What are you talking about?"

"Once the word got out we have a new little Galloway, the whole family wanted to meet him at once. Doesn't that make sense? That way, we'll all have known him for the same length of time."

"I just don't want the little guy to be overwhelmed."

"Sorry to give you the news, but they have endless energy at this age. I'm more worried about you."

Gage and Wyatt had almost reached the bonfire when he heard voices coming from a barn that was a distance away. The barn's huge door lifted open and a tractor with a wagon behind it pulled out. Adults and children were arranged in the wagon as if they were having a hayride. The adults and a young girl sat on hay bales, and there were younger children sitting on laps.

Trey and Max took off running toward the wagon, with Bree in close pursuit along with another woman Gage presumed was Wyatt's wife Kristin. He should know his family better, but dusk was already on the horizon, so he couldn't worry about who he didn't recognize.

There was a lot of hubbub surrounding the best method of getting the family members in the wagon out and onto solid ground. Wyatt said that he wanted to make things easier for Trey, and so he named Leo as the ad hoc master of ceremonies. As families were unloaded from the wagon, Leo would announce the names and introduce them.

The first ones who came off the wagon were Gage's brother Caleb and his wife Annie, in addition to Chloe, Annie's eight-year-old daughter.

After Chole was helped down from the wagon, she produced a big box from behind her back. "Trey, I love you so much." The girl hugged Trey with her free arm, then led him over to a picnic table. The little boy ripped open the package, and Max joined in tearing off the last pieces. Bree had the boys stand back while she popped the lid off the box, pulled a junior-sized cowboy hat out, and placed it on their son's head.

That was the cutest thing ever, and after the child had waited so long for him to be with Gage's side of his family, too.

*Thank you, Lord.*

# Chapter 18

Bree couldn't take her eyes off of Trey, strutting around on the Galloway Sons Farm in his own cowboy hat that fit him perfectly. Her little boy may have thrust his chest out a bit, he was so proud. She had hoped and prayed for Trey to meet his family. Tears pricked the back of her eyes. Once the others had unloaded from the wagon, more gifts were handed to Trey. Leo handed him a gift that turned out to be a small canvas with a scene of the Galloway Sons on it, the sky all purples, pinks, and oranges.

"You can hang that in your room and know where you come from." Trey ran and gave the art to Bree, then ran back for more gifts. She heaved a sigh of relief his talented uncle's gift hadn't been damaged.

Trey unwrapped Wyatt's gift, which was a miniature solar

windmill. "This is a wind turbine. Now depending on how fast the wind is blowing, these blades will generate a certain amount of solar energy that runs things like your air conditioner." Trey studied Wyatt as he spoke, and put his hand on his uncle's sleeve.

Caleb came next and handed Trey what turned out to be a small barn. "This is a replica of what we're building at the farm, Trey. I hope you'll come visit when the workers are there if you want to."

"I do!"

Trey brought the gifts to her.

The gifting over, Trey went running off a short distance with Max. A small fence around the exterior of the bonfire made her feel better about the fire being so close.

A woman came up to her and Bree glimpsed a western-styled top flowed over her modest baby bump. "Welcome to the family. I'm Annie." Everyone in town knew Annie York had married Gage's brother Caleb after he'd been granted full custody of his twin babies, a niece and nephew. Annie had come up from behind and she patted Bree's elbow. "You couldn't be in a more kind, accomplished, faith-filled family, at least that's what they've been for me."

But Bree wasn't in the family. Trey was. She was deciding whether to clear that up with Annie when another woman approached them with a child on each hip, one a boy and one a girl. Each wore a tiny cowboy hat and T-shirt with a cowboy on it or a cowgirl on it.

"Hi, I'm Kayla. I'm the baby sister to the wild Galloway Sons.

And this is Ella and Drew. They're mine."

The smile on the woman's face and her attitude conveyed that being her kids' mom was the best thing in the world, and Bree gave a little tug to Drew's knee. "They're adorable. I'm sure they keep you plenty busy."

Kayla nodded. "We climbed in the wagon last because these two got into mommy's face cream and slathered it all over them. I had to wash them up before we came."

Annie laughed.

They acted like she was one of them and she would be. "Thanks for the warm welcome into the family. I'm looking forward to getting to know you all better."

Annie nodded. "We know we can be a lot, especially all at once. But we're just so thrilled for Gage to be a dad. You and Trey are going to be good for him. You already are."

What was she supposed to say to that? When the conversation moved along, she realized they weren't looking for her input. They'd stated what they saw as facts.

"Trey's a handsome kid," Kayla said. "We always have room for a new addition. Or more than one." Gage's sister exchanged a look with Annie, and Bree wondered what it'd be like to be sisters-in-law with these sweet, beautiful women.

She *did* know that everyone was trying to make her feel at home, and she felt it. Given that she hadn't married into the family, and hadn't told them about Trey until he was five, they were all as nice as they could be. She shot up a prayer of thanks.

"Is this meeting for women-only?" Gage came up beside Bree

with Trey by his side. He looked like a new man, the lines of tension in his face all smoothed out. He gave her a relaxed smile. Trey stood in between the two of them. Gage reached his hands out and wiggled his fingers toward Drew. "Come here, buddy. We men need to stick together."

Drew buried his face in his mother's shoulder. Kayla coaxed him to look at his uncle, and then he tossed Gage a slight smile before he went to his uncle.

Gage turned toward their son. "Drew is another one of your cousins, Trey. Would you like to get to know him better? He's going to look up to a big boy like you one day."

The child nodded. Gage led the way as he showed Trey a wooden rocking chair and told him to take a seat. Gage then set his little cousin beside him and gently put the rocker in motion, while he stood very close.

Gage's attitude, of prioritizing the human connections, was contagious. She felt her muscles loosen and her heart rate, which had been galloping due to all the excitement, slowed. This was what it was all about. Cousins knowing one another. Family being there. All of these busy people had cleared their schedules to make her son feel at home.

Kristin walked up from around the driveway off the house. "Sorry I'm late. Half out the door and somebody needed a diaper change. Happened twice." She'd brought her stroller for triplets and the three babies were bundled in it. Their personalities were starting to show. Keith had the strongest resemblance to Trey at that age, his hair wavy and dark, with a little button nose and rosy cheeks. His face brightened when he caught sight of Bree. She couldn't resist giving his chin a little tweak. Everyone gathered around and Leo took over managing the stroller while Kristin helped create a line to put the hotdogs on the wire spikes in a mass production line.

It was simple fare and went surprisingly quickly with so many hands to help distribute the hotdogs on buns, condiments, potato salad and baked beans. Then it was time to roast marshmallows, and the adults did all the cooking, except for Chloe, who seemed to enjoy turning her black marshmallow into soot.

Trey and Max were running around under Sierra's watchful eye when Wyatt clanked a fork on a cocoa mug. "I want to introduce you all to somebody." For the first time, Bree noticed a man she'd never see before standing by Wyatt. "This is Miles Galloway, our cousin. We knew him when we were little kids. Not to get into my whole history, but most of you know, when I was a teen living away from the farm, far from Fair Creek, I lived with Miles and his family. We started Vortex Clean Energy together and then I bought him out." He stopped, like he was letting all of that sink in. "Well, Miles and I have been in touch lately. He wanted to come and meet our newest member, Trey."

A patter of clapping went up from the small group.

Miles stepped forward. "I have such fond memories of you all. It's always good to get back to family. Trey, I'd like to give you something."

Trey went bounding up, with Max coming up right behind him. Miles handed Trey a jersey from the sports team from his state.

"Mommy, I got a shirt!" Trey yelled so loud everyone could hear him.

Miles, who had stepped away from the center of attention after giving the shirt, returned to the spotlight. "Trey's reminded me that I want to give an especially warm welcome to his mom, Bree. You're one of us now, Bree."

The man not only had the Galloways' good looks, he had their warmth for others.

Without overthinking it, Bree lifted her arm high in the air and waved so everyone could see she was grateful.

The applause in response to Miles's announcement was louder than any before, with a couple of whoops and hollers added in. Gage had stood beside her during the announcements and now put his fingers to his lips to give an old-fashioned whistle like he used to do when they were at ballgames in school.

She smiled to herself, feeling hidden in the early evening darkness. This must be how it felt to have her cup running over, her heart filled to the brim. She inhaled the scent of wheat fields and the smokiness of the burning wood, and a hint of Gage's aftershave. She didn't know what the future held but she trusted God would make it work for her good and Trey's.

When Gage slipped his arm around her shoulders, she couldn't resist snuggling into his chest, and murmured in his ear. "You have a beautiful family, Gage. I'm so blessed to be a part of it."

Gage guided her to step away a short distance from the others.

They were so close his eyes sparkled through the darkness. "You've finally seen the light, darling. Be warned though, Galloways are bound together for life."

Bree's shoulders tensed. unsure if she was ready to give up control. She swallowed. "Kind of like grey wolves?"

He loosened his arm from her shoulders, and quirked an eyebrow. "What are you talking about?"

She shrugged. "Trey's studying the habits of various mammals at preschool. The male and female grey wolves who lead the pack mate for life."

He directed his words into her ear, imitating a growl. "I like the sound of that."

When Gage brought her closer still, Bree hoped he couldn't feel how rapidly her heart was beating. "I'll admit to being alarmed to the idea at first," she said. "But I've started to think being committed for life, the way we are to Trey, may be what's best."

"That's the right answer," he said, the corners of his mouth turned up. "Now, look for the Galloway family coat of arms to come in the mail. You can put it on your wall."

"I've got a nice spot in the back of the museum's garage," she deadpanned.

His lips were inches from hers. "I'm afraid I've corrupted you with my teasing ways, darling."

"As long as you keep loving Trey the way you are, I'll handle anything you dish out."

He locked his gaze on hers. When he brushed his lips over

hers, Bree's breath caught in her throat. He tasted of marshmallows and coffee, and what sparked between them seemed brighter than any bonfire. He deepened the kiss, and she slipped her arms around his neck.

Time stood still as they couldn't get enough of one another, but it had to have been less than a minute when Gage pulled away. Both of them were breathing harder than before. He nuzzled her ear. "I hate to interrupt what we're doing, but Annie'll probably want to take Max home soon so we better go get Trey."

Bree nodded. Trey. She needed to think about Trey. She couldn't remember him being out of her mind like this since he was born.

Gage set off toward the house. She followed, wondering what she had done, kissing Gage like that? Except, he'd been the one to start it.

She had certainly been a full participant. Her face flushed thinking about it.

But then she felt a calm that could only come from the one who stilled the seas. Her attitude shifted and instead of focusing on what she was missing, she intentionally appreciated all that she had. A load had been lifted from her. Even though things in the past hadn't turned out the way she wanted, which was to rear her child while married, she intended to be grateful for what she had.

Why did she have the feeling she was about to have a whole lot more?

That kiss must have done more than awaken her senses. It must have drained her mind of any logical thought.

# Chapter 19

The morning after the bonfire to welcome Trey, Gage stared out the kitchen window at the farmland where the horizon stretched out before him. He'd never felt so connected to his roots than now as he stood on the ground he'd been raised on.

Last night, seeing all of his family together to support him, Trey, and Bree, had touched him more deeply than he expected. So many thoughts swirled. He tore his gaze from the fields, pulled on his cowboy boots, and went to start his chores, since the dark of night had fully lifted. On his walk to the barn, the sunlight shone through the tree leaves above his head, like he was following a yellow brick road. Apparently, the secret to getting up early was kissing a beautiful woman the night before.

A knot formed in his stomach. It had been great to share

that kiss with Bree. But since they had so much between them as friends and now co-parents, the situation was complicated. And their philosophies about preserving history and looking to the future were out of alignment. He'd tossed and turned into the wee hours and had been more than ready to start his day when the alarm rang.

Gage pulled open the barn door and but the glimpse of the sheer beauty of rows of golden corn stalks stopped him in his tracks. He didn't go in and just appreciated the view. Bree must be getting to him. He had never admired something growing in the ground in his life. He ducked inside, heard Louise's whinny, and enjoyed her greeting, only he frowned a moment later. Would what happened last night cost him his friendship with Bree? She'd seemed as involved in the kiss as he was, but sometimes women saw things differently.

Phoebe had been that way. But he wasn't going to drag up old feelings from a couple years ago. No need to think about how he'd been planning to propose marriage when she'd broken it off with him. He grumbled under his breath as he went about taking care of Louise. One thing about the monotony of caring for animals was it was mindless and soothing. He picked up a shovel and fell into a rhythm, and before he knew it, he was mucking out the last stall.

Kissing Bree had been the best idea ever, and he wanted to spend more time with her doing more of the same. He broke into a smile thinking about her.

The manure piled up as he worked, giving off a rank odor.

It was unbelievable that decades ago, he'd left this all behind, determined never to come back. He'd devoted himself to his life's work.

He still couldn't quite believe the call had come in from Caleb to return home and run the farm for a time. Dad's will had said every brother had to be involved to inherit their portion. An ache in his gut came out of nowhere. If he were ever meant to spend time at the farm, he wished it had happened when Dad was alive. He'd been closer to Dad than any of his siblings. Everyone in his family had wanted to be better understood by their father. Gage had wanted to understand Dad better. He still did.

He finished up, showered, and took extra care shaving and chose a nicer shirt than usual. Spending the day with Bree was worth extra effort, and he'd be seeing Trey, too. He'd never thought of himself as a role model but now he was starting to.

At the agreed-upon time, Gage stood on the porch at the museum before it even opened to the public, and called Bree on his cell. He was as nervous as a schoolboy, shuffling from one foot to the other.

The phone rang twice and he thought for a minute she wasn't going to pick up. Then her sweet voice came over the line. "Hi, I'll come down and let you in."

"Great, I thought for a minute I'd have to see if you'd let your hair down for me to climb up."

She giggled and through the phone, he heard her open a door, which meant she was coming from the apartment into the museum part. She didn't hang up and stayed on the line.

"We've already had our first crisis of the day," she said.

Before he could ask for the details the museum's outer door opened, and Bree stood in front of him, holding her phone up to her ear. She flashed him a smile and hung up. So did he. She tugged on his sleeve pulled him inside. The fruity smell of her hair, something mango and strawberry, surrounded her. How would he work with her all day, when picking up where they left off last night kept running through his mind?

"Hey, Gage. How's it going?" Kristin came into the main room, from out of nowhere.

They weren't alone.

Gage felt the weight of disappointment more than he expected. "Well, I haven't been accosted by a Murphite so far." He'd thought the day would start out with just the two of them.

Bree shot out an answer. "Don't get discouraged. I'm sure we can arrange something."

Kristin ran her fingers through her long reddish hair. "Actually, we have something to ask you. "

Bree interrupted her. "No. Don't bring it up."

Kristin went on anyway. "We don't think you'll be thrilled about it but hope you'll take one for the team."

"I've never been into sports but okay, go with it."

Kristin paced around the room. "We've been keeping it a secret because we were going to have the big reveal. But a celebrity who knew Dale Murphy was supposed to be the grand marshal of the festival parade. Her people just called and she's too sick to come. She's devastated, but these people are in the 80s or older, since Dale's been gone a while now. We knew it was a risk."

It was the first day of a three-day festival so he had some time and could make this happen and find somebody good for them. "I'll work the phone for you and find someone else you think could fill such an important role," he teased.

Bree picked up a pen on the desk and doodled. "It's not going to be that easy. The festival means something to a lot of people and they like all the details."

"Sorry. I didn't mean anything by implying a substitute would be easy to find."

Bree charged on. "Apology accepted. But if this festival dies out, how will we fund all our charities and organizations? See, every kid who parks cars at the school needs a crowd because the fee to park buys sports uniforms."

He went over and stood by Bree. "I've been away for all these years, and keeping the festival going has been on your plate.

"The parade's this afternoon. Will you do it?"

Gage couldn't believe what he was hearing. But it seemed like a small request, all things considered. "I don't think of myself as a celebrity. What all's involved?"

Kristin's eyes lit up. "We've got a classic car you ride in. You might get interviewed by the press. It's sort of like you're the star of the day. People might come and shake your hand."

Bree went over, flipped a switch and the case that held Dale's saddle, chaps and other items lit up. "You'll feel great about yourself, and if you ever wanted to be a celebrity, the grand marshal gig will give you a taste of it."

One of his favorite things about his work was fading into the background and giving his subject the spotlight. "I'd rather sign up for an invisible cloak, darling. You couldn't reach me in the past because I stayed under the radar, to give others a voice when they needed it."

Flashbacks of times their approaches were dissimilar came to mind. On projects, he coped with humor, and she knuckled down, became a control freak, and didn't find anything he said funny. They'd partnered on a project in government class, and the senior class picnic committee nearly collapsed because of them. They hadn't been good with compromise back then.

"Really, I had no idea." Bree's phone alarm went off. "Ten-minute warning. It's almost show time," she said, her mouth in a rigid line.

Gage went over to a clipboard where she had listed judges for various events, the bands that would play, and more. "Looks like everything's in order."

Bree looked up, but it was as though she didn't see him, her eyes flitted away so quickly. He touched her arm in the lightest way possible. "This is a big day. What can I do to help you?"

Her pen continued to move down the page. But he wasn't going to move his hand until she showed she wanted him to. Finally, she got to the bottom of the page and lifted him away to turn the page.

"Actually, just having you here, for moral support, means a lot. Would you mind if we took a moment for a silent prayer?"

Gage wasn't sure what he'd expected, but this seemed like

progress. "Of course."

For around a minute or minute and a half, they stood together with their eyes closed. So did Kristin. Gage just rested his mind, not really sure how to pray for her. God knew her needs, just as he knew Gage's own.

When she was ready, she opened her eyes and gave him a smile that he knew was genuine. "I'm going to unlock the exterior door so visitors can come in. I'm feeling better now. Thank you. You're going to make an incredible grand marshal. You'll see."

Gage wasn't so sure.

# Chapter 20

Bree unlocked the museum door and let the early Dale Murphy fans come in, then let out the breath she'd been holding. When she'd answered the door earlier and seen Gage, it took all her willpower not to throw her arms around his neck and pick up where they'd left off.

A text pinged on her phone. It was Jo sending her a "good luck" message with a smiley face. Bree hit "heart" in response, grateful to focus her thoughts away from Gage.

They were friends, and that's how they needed to stay, right?

More messages came, one from the president of the Murphites fan club. Her tension converted to excitement as friends and the star's fans texted her that they were at the festival and the parking spots were filling up.

The way Gage's coloring had turned pink when she pushed

him about being grand marshal nagged at her. Mainly, she blamed herself for pushing him too far. This wasn't his festival, and he wasn't even her boyfriend. How had things gone so wrong? Especially when all she'd wanted to do when she woke up this morning was to see him and work the festival. And have another luscious kiss.

"I came to compete in the Dale Murphy Lookalike Contest." A young woman in her thirties stood at the museum's counter where Bree rang up two of the newly designed T-shirts, one each for her and her husband.

"That's wonderful. I see the resemblance, now that you mention it. There's a brochure in the bag that has the weekend schedule."

The couple ducked into the exhibits, and Bree organized some of the bills in her cash drawer before looking up to see the next fan who'd come to visit. Gage stood in front of her, with Trey by his side, and both beamed at her.

"Hi, Mommy. Daddy said we could come and see you and we don't have to buy anything. But I like buying. And it helps you."

She wasn't going to get into an economics lesson with her five-year-old today. "Do what your daddy says. He's a smart man, honey." It was Bree's turn to blush when she looked into Gage's dark-brown eyes that were creamy, like butterscotch. If he was angry, she couldn't tell. He seemed the opposite, like maybe he was falling for her like she had for him.

She noted Kristin was covering the other register and Bree had a gap in customers. "Your daddy's also kind and warm. He's also funny."

"You didn't seem to think so earlier."

Trey's innocent face made Bree even more conscious of Gage and what a good man he was. Handsome, too. "Surely, you know that sometimes, I'm not in the mood for teasing," she said.

"I guess I'd forgotten, darling. It's been years, you know."

On impulse, she threw aside her misgivings, wanting to find their way back to last night. "Trey, would you go over and help Aunt Kristin at her register? I need Daddy's help for a minute in the other room."

"Yes, Mommy. Then I wanna go ride on the golf cart again."

"Okay, you can do that if he okays it, honey."

Gage simply gave Trey a thumbs-up. Trey grinned.

Bree watched that Trey had safely connected with Kristin in the noisy, crowded room. Then she locked up her register, tucked her hand into Gage's, and led him to the business part of the museum.

The volunteers were all out on the floor, and the quiet was a relief she hadn't known she needed. She still held Gage's hand in hers and nothing had felt so right.

"You don't have to tend to me. I'm fine," Gage said.

She pulled him into the closet with the cleaning supplies, which wasn't an ideal fit for two people. "Well, *I'm* not fine," Bree said. "Kiss me, Gage, if you wouldn't mind."

His mouth was warm and ready for hers, and it was like fireworks shooting off. She hadn't dreamed it. They had reacted to one another in a new way, a way that seemed nothing like friends.

He wrapped his arm around her waist, and her hands were touching his face when she reluctantly pulled away. "I've gotta get back to work."

He kissed her again. "Okay, just don't forget about me. And remember humor is my default behavior. I apologize ahead of time."

She latched onto his elbow. "Your default mode is better than most people's go-to move. Now, I'm going to work and will come meet you and Trey at the kiddie tractor pull."

Moments later, when they reentered the retail area, it was so crowded no one had missed them.

More than an hour later, Bree waited at her register for the assigned volunteer to relieve her.

"How's it going?" Jo approached her with a small, insulated food bag. "I brought you a snack, Bree. Figured you could use it. From my upstairs window, the number of visitors looks much larger than last year, so it's going to be crazy. Better go have some fun."

Bree sold a mini notebook with Dale Murphy on the cover to a little girl dressed up like the movie star. "I'll check it out when I walk down to the fire station parking lot and see Trey in the mini tractor pull."

Jo handed Bree the snack bag. "Better get going. I'm filling in for you. Natalie from church is sick."

"I don't feel right about leaving you here with this crowd."

"I'll be just fine, Breezy. Elizabeth is coming to relieve me.

There's an estate auction I'll be going to in a couple of hours. Trey needs his mommy to be with him, with the changes in his life. I'm thinking Gage might miss you too."

Bree scooted away to avoid a discussion on Gage she wasn't prepared for. As she walked along Main Street, she munched on her cheese sticks and Triscuits. Townspeople and strangers were at the lemon shakeup stand, getting elephant ears, and in line for the rides. When she reached the tractor pull, it was like a Galloway Sons reunion.

She couldn't wipe the smile from her face, and Trey ran and hugged her. "Mommy, my family came to watch me."

Bree shot up a prayer of thanks for all the attention Trey was getting. He had done many things alone for years, with her as his only cheerleader. Her heart was full to the limit, she was so happy for him.

Gage came up to them, and when he didn't give her a kiss, she understood. She tried to hide her disappointment with a big grin. Wyatt and Sierra were getting Max ready to compete. The tractors were all the right size for children to ride. When Gage helped Trey to settle into the little green tractor, Bree tossed up a prayer of thanks.

Over the next hour, the whole family cheered for all the kids, including others who weren't their own.

And Gage moved closer to Bree, as if he couldn't resist her. When she saw his cowboy hat dip down as he made a move to kiss her, she met him halfway. "Let's kiss like nobody's watching," he said in her ear.

A shiver went up her spine. She glanced at all the visitors, some dressed in skirts from the Dale Murphy era, others simply mothers and dads with big smiles as they pulled kids in wagons down the closed-off streets. "Pretty sure no one will notice if we do."

"So here's another thing we agree on," he said. His kiss wasn't much more than a peck, since they were walking. Bree was almost as warmed inside as their first time though. Her shoulders loosened and she inhaled the scent of fried food and popcorn.

"I could get used to this," she said. They reached a place where they were in synch somehow and accepted that their different perspectives were okay.

The Galloways made quite the sight walking together through the festival. They all talked, some broke away and ate, and others tried the rides. Gage, Bree, and Trey did it all. In the Tilt-a-Whirl ride, they shrieked and giggled their way through, with the motion slamming them into one another as they went. Trey shrieked the whole time, and Bree and Gage enjoyed being so close, sneaking kisses over his head when they could.

"It's the most fun I've had," she admitted to Gage, almost stumbling from motion sickness.

He pulled off a bite of cotton candy from the stick that Caleb had held for them, placed it in his mouth, and showed her his blue tongue after it melted. "You've been saying that. But I'm offering to help you have many more good times in your future," he said. The man had a way with words, that was for sure.

"Don't make promises you can't keep, Parade Marshal Man."

He looked her in the eye, and his expression was unreadable. It was as if they'd gotten a little loopy together and didn't know where they'd end up.

Just as Bree was trying to find the will to go back to work, Kristin texted her and said all bases were covered and she wasn't needed. She suspected the whole town was covering at the museum to give her a date night, and for once she wasn't bothered by their interference.

A little while later, she was walking with Gage and Trey in the park, content and distracted by the vintage cars, when she remembered the time. "I'm sorry that I've made you do this, but it's time to get in place for the parade."

Gage checked his phone. "But we've got an hour yet."

"You make it sound like you're going to serve time."

"Hey, can I have your autograph?" Wyatt had come up beside them.

"What do you think?" Gage's attitude made Bree feel worse, but Gage hooked his arm loosely around her shoulders, caught hold of Trey's hand, and they all veered off and headed to where Kristin had told him to line up.

They'd walked a little ways in silence before Gage spoke. "Hey, wanna ride in the classic car with me, buddy?"

Trey pumped his fist in the air. "Yes!"

"I don't know if that's a good idea, and he'll miss them tossing candy along the parade route."

Gage quirked an eyebrow. "Want to throw out candy to your friends, Trey?"

The boy nodded. "You too, Mommy."

Gage grinned at her as if he'd won a victory, which he had. "If I've gotta do this, so do you. Will you join us?"

The hour waiting for the floats, tractors, and those on horseback to line up went quickly as Gage told jokes that kept Trey laughing. The clowns came over and made balloon animals for the kids waiting to be in the parade.

Once the three of them were in the car, they were off. Kristin must have coached the announcer on Gage's background because he outlined his many achievements when he introduced him. The kids went a little wild, possibly wanting candy, but it was still nice. Then they were underway. Sitting beside Gage and Trey as they rode along at a snail's pace proved to be a special pleasure.

"Now, just a few pieces at a time, buddy."

Bree inhaled Gage's scent as they sat thigh to thigh on the front seat of the small-sized car with Trey. "You've got secret talents, Gage. You're an expert in candy tossing 101."

"We've had this conversation before, darling. Don't think you know everything there is to know about me."

Bree reached into the bucket of candy. "Oh, I don't. I'm enjoying finding out more though." She threw out a few little suckers toward two sisters that were elementary school-aged and dressed like Dale Murphy.

The car finally got near the end of the parade route where Ted Mitchell waved to them from the judges' podium. Bree heaved a sigh that the judges were all in their places.

The Galloways met up at the town firemen's tent where they

bought hamburgers and managed to snag a picnic table to sit for several minutes.

Then it was time for the 50s dance competition. Kayla's twins, Ella and Drew, had their own dance off in the far corner of the parking lot stage. Even the triplet babies were shaking their little selves to the music, under Leo's watchful eye.

Midway through the dancing, Annie and Chloe left without explanation. Chloe returned dressed like Dale Murphy and could even repeat a few lines. She placed second in the children's category of the lookalike contest.

The adult look-alike contest wasn't so low-key. There were boos afterward.

Gage leaned close to Bree's ear as they watched in lawn chairs they'd brought from the car. "Isn't this contest supposed to be for fun?"

She whispered back. "The Murphites take all of this very seriously."

The crowds from each event seemed to build and move along to each event throughout the day. By evening, Bree and Gage were figuring out how to get Trey home and in bed. Bree's cell phone rang.

"The electricity is off at the stage." Jo was unflappable and showed no hint of panic.

Bree tried to match her calm and failed. "What? The band is what caps off the day. I'm not sure what to do."

"Well, head over to the stage and go from there."

Bree's emotions had been running high all day, and she'd

kept it together. But the problem with the sound and having the largest audience ever to watch it was testing her self-control.

Bree explained the situation to Gage, and he picked up Trey, who was drooping like a sunflower late in the season, and carried him. "Maybe I can help. I'm pretty good with troubleshooting mechanical issues, darling."

Bree could barely keep up with his long strides. "You are? You'd do that for me?" she choked out.

"What have I been telling you?"

"About not knowing you?"

Gage's finger was surprisingly soft as he brushed her cheek. "I'd do anything for you, darling."

When they arrived at their destination, the number of people in lawn chairs and the bleachers at the stage was massive. The Twisted Nails were one of the more popular bands in the area. The eight o'clock start time had come and gone, and many had used the time waiting to chat with others in the crowd.

Gage went over to where two men were clustered around the stage trying to sort the electricity. Bree stayed with him, in case Trey woke up. She also wanted to see Gage in action.

"Can I take a look?" he said.

She had no idea if he'd be able to do anything and wondered why he'd try. Plus, what did those words even mean? Were they only meant to be applied to machinery?

Wyatt and Sierra came up to the stage. "We dropped off Max with Aunt Elizabeth and came to hear some music," she said.

Wyatt must have read Bree's thoughts. "When it comes to

all things mechanical, you can trust Gage to get the job done. We'll say a little prayer things get repaired quickly. But in the meantime, keep the faith."

The minutes ticked on as Gage worked, and some in the crowd packed up and left. It was forty-five minutes past the start time.

Even Gage didn't look as cool as he had when they got there. But that made it all the sweeter when he fixed the problem and the band began warming up. Bree kissed Gage and didn't care who saw her.

She was sure her face was pink when she pulled away. Several people in the audience whistled.

Wyatt had remained close by. "Hey, I felt like kissing him too, but I'm glad you beat me to it. I'm sure he is too."

It was a great end to a glorious day. Kristin phoned in to say they'd sold merchandise in record numbers. The special purse had sold, and Kristin kept a photo of it so that others had placed orders.


Back at her place, Gage and Bree put Trey to bed. The sandman visited him immediately, and Gage wrapped his arm around Bree's waist as they went into her living room.

Bree couldn't control a huge yawn, and Gage studied her. "You look a little pale. You must be exhausted."

"I'm okay." She couldn't muster up the energy to sound convincing.

Gage kissed her, and the sensations went down to her toes.

He pulled away too soon. "It's going to be hard to leave you and Trey when I go to DC." He hesitated. "I'm going to miss you."

She'd never had trouble sorting out her feelings, but she was all over the place. "I wish you didn't have to go." That much was true. But she'd also like to get off this roller coaster ride of emotions when he was around.

He hesitated, as if he might have expected her to say more. She didn't, and he continued. "This is so new, the change in our relationship. Will you be here for me when I get back?"

"Of course. We'll be here. I just need some time I guess."

"I could say more, but I don't want to scare you off, Bree."

What did he mean? Her heart rate went up a notch. She wouldn't be sharing her deep, personal thoughts, if she'd known them. He knew that about her, and he wasn't much better.

Gage kissed her again, and it was bittersweet—a goodbye kiss for sure. Sweet but not so intense. He stood, and she rallied her energy to walk him to the door.

"Can I call and talk to Trey?"

This was safe territory, and she grabbed onto it like a lifeline. "He'd really like that."

"Sleep well, sweet Bree. Take care while I'm gone." Then he left, and she locked the door and headed upstairs, fighting a strong desire to go after him. But she needed to be grateful. Things were moving too quickly.

Weren't they?

# Chapter 21

Gage was pretty sure he was in culture shock as he sat on the Galloway Sons Farm private jet on their airstrip in the back of the property. Being with Bree and Trey had been more than he'd hoped for. Now that the Dale Murphy Festival had ended, he found himself replaying certain memories in his mind.

"Are you ready for take-off, sir?"

"You can call me Gage," he told the pilot and the crew member standing nearby. "Yes, if you think everything's in order, I'm ready."

He hadn't been totally truthful. He was physically packed but not mentally ready. He didn't want to leave Indiana, and that hadn't happened to him before. So this was new, feeling like he didn't want to go in to work.

He settled in and looked over his materials to prepare for the meeting. Before he knew it, he'd landed in D.C. The hustle and bustle of cities had always given him energy. Not this time. He wanted to get in and get out. He wasn't totally sure why. But he'd seen Trey every day since he found out he was a dad. He already missed the little guy.

And he couldn't begin to sort out how he felt about Bree. He knew one thing: God had done as he'd prayed, and any bitterness he'd felt about losing time with Trey was gone. He would never forget, but he could forgive, and he had. He was still working on forgiving himself for his part in what happened.

His days in D.C. were full, and he was grateful. Last night, he called Bree and Trey, but it felt odd not to be with them. He didn't like the distance of the phones between them.

On the second night, his phone rang. It was Bree. "How are you, Gage?"

"I'm about as you'd think, darling. Missing Trey something fierce. Can you put him on?" He missed her too, but it was still all so new.

"I'm sorry. He crashed early, and you said meetings today would go late anyway."

"True. What about you? How was your day?"

"Fine, but I didn't call to make small talk." She sounded like she was on edge or something.

His grip on the phone tightened. "I don't mind it, but I've had a long day, so we can skip the chatter if you want to. You have a way of dropping life-changing news, darling. So why don't you just tell me?"

"Remember that photo you found at the museum? You noticed two people with a resemblance to your family."

His mind raced ahead. He didn't know why he was jumping to conclusions, but Bree didn't do anything partway. She was generally calm. "Sure, I do. Everybody has doppelgangers. I looked a lot like a guy in college, especially if our hair was cut a certain way and we happened to dress alike."

Why was he making excuses? *Listen to what she has to say, Gage.*

"Well, you wanted a forensics expert to look, but I'm into genealogy and saw it as a challenge. I subscribe to a magazine that teaches all kinds of research techniques on how to find things out. It's really interesting. I think you'd enjoy—"

"Passing time with you is always a pleasure, darling. I'm not sure that I'd be interested in studying my family tree, but I've never tried it. Uh, the suspense is killing me. What's going on? Does this have something to do with Trey?"

"So, to relax after the festival, I decided to do this exercise the magazine described. On the cover it said, 'Find Your Ancestor in a Week: Seven Easy Tips.' Actually, you were supposed to take one full day to do each step. But, since I needed something intense to unwind, I got so involved I finished in record time."

"I love overachievers. And especially how enthusiastic you are, darling. What'd you find out?"

"First, I did some digging, and a notebook at my museum showed who had donated that photo. It was the Weaver family, and they'd named the people in the photo but hadn't written that on the back of it."

"That's huge, Bree. Having a name makes it much simpler, from what little I know about it."

"Well, I think it would be better for you to know a little more. Plus, it's fascinating, Gage. It really is. As part of my work at the museum, sometimes I've helped people find out things about their family histories. I will call larger institutions for data.

"So, there are census records and birth certificates and marriage licenses, all kinds of public records to help. The magazine talked about searching occupations and military service. Anyway, that photo, I'm fairly certain, they are your half brothers. Having an unusual name makes it a little easier to track somebody down. One of the Weaver sons is named Gage. That's his middle name, just like your dad's. It appears your dad was stationed at an air force base in Tennessee. He had a girlfriend who delivered twin babies long after they broke up. Based on her death certificate and your mom and dad's marriage license, I've verified it."

She finally stopped talking, and Gage wasn't sure how he wanted to fill the gap. "How did Trey do on his quiz about sea otters?"

There was a pause, and he supposed she didn't know how to deal with his avoiding the subject. "The quiz was today," she said. "So he hasn't heard back yet. Thanks for studying with him."

"I think the novelty of studying by phone the way we did might've helped him."

"Gage, I'm sorry if I've upset you. Learning this has had an impact on me, ever since I found out. If it wasn't so hard to believe. And certainly disturbing, in its own way."

She didn't tell him about them, and I'm not sure of the circumstances. Her death certificate showed she died very young. I have a feeling she didn't have the chance to tell her sons who their father was."

Gage's thoughts were all over the place. "That's quite the tale you're telling."

"I know, and I'm sorry. I suppose I should have waited until you came home."

He was home, or at least DC was where he'd be working in journalism for the foreseeable future. That didn't seem an important point to make. Why couldn't he focus?

"Are you still there, Gage?"

"I am. I have no idea what to say." It was the second time in his life he'd been unable to find words. And both times had been within the past few weeks. Also, both times had involved Bree Murphy.

"I'm beginning to wonder if I should limit my time with you, Bree. You're bringing an excessive amount of drama."

"I feel like you think it's easy for me, to be on the end of always delivering dramatic news. It isn't. I'm left wondering how to make things better. Believe me, Gage, the last thing I want to do is bring these situations to you. Really. But you deserve to know. And I want you to talk to me, about all of it, of course. I hope to talk with you more and more, to get back to how it was when we were in school. We never ran out of conversation."

After talking about the small talk they said they wouldn't, Gage said good night and hung up.

Somehow, he thought he had another sleepless night ahead of him. He'd wanted to understand Dad better, and now he would possibly do that. But it would be under a circumstance he didn't want any part of.

As the eldest, it might make sense this knowledge had found him first. He could check it out, and if it turned out to be true, he could bring the information to the others. But he'd just gotten back into the family and begun to get a little comfortable, and he might have to shake all of that up, depending on what news he came up with.

# Chapter 22

Bree settled back in the black limo and tried to relax as Galloway Sons farmland went by her window. The cornstalks and soybeans in the fields would be harvested any day now. With all the changes in her life, she welcomed a front-row seat for the continuity of the seasons. Things in the greater world were how they'd always been. But her world had tilted on its axis, in a good way.

"What do ya think, buddy?" Gage sat on the other side of the back seat, and Trey was in between them.

"It's really cool."

Bree smoothed his cowlick away. "There' so many more words to describe it, honey. You may not have the vocabulary now, but someday you will. These are black leather seats. It's an expensive car and gives a smooth ride." She didn't know why she was pushing this on a five-year-old, but the effort was never wasted. He was a sponge.

Gage caught her eye from above Trey's head. "Mommy's right, Trey. We're taking you on a big boy trip, and we hope you'll enjoy it. But we also have business to take care of and people to meet. You think you can hang in for all this?"

The boy nodded. "Yes, Daddy."

The car pulled up to a place on the airstrip, and the driver put it into park and came around and opened the doors. "Be careful going up the steps, guys. Have a safe trip. See you when you get back."

"Thanks for the ride." Seemed silly, but it never hurt to be grateful.

Gage slipped the driver some bills and came up beside her. "I'm so glad you two are coming with me. It's another one of your brilliant ideas."

"Mixing business and pleasure is parenting at its best, I've always said." She had to catch her breath at the luxury of it all. And the familiar scent of his aftershave had her wondering how they might sneak some time together.

With the driver getting their luggage out, all they had to do was climb up the stairs and get on.

She flashed Gage a smile. "This is the way to travel. I've got just one question. Where've you been all my life?"

He laughed, the same sound she'd heard all through her childhood. He kept her grounded in reality somehow. "Not close enough to you, darling."

They walked onto the plane, and Trey ran to a window to look out. "Stay with Mommy, Trey."

"He'll be fine," Gage assured her. "That's what's great about a private jet. No other passengers to worry about. Security is airtight. You can relax." He directed her to her seat and guided Trey to his, then sat down across from them. "Easy for you to say when I'm the one who dug up the info that's taking us to Tennessee. What if I've made a mistake? Or what if I'm right, but you wish I'd never uncovered Cameron and Clint?"

Leaning forward, Gage studied her, his dark-brown eyes seeming to see her for the first time. Drawn to him, she automatically leaned out from her seat and bridged the gap between them. To her surprise, he kissed her, and his lips, firm and warm on hers, cleared out every thought except him. He reached for her hair, and she reveled in his affection.

"Mommy." Trey poked her arm. "Can I have gum?"

Gage drew back from her. "I've got it." He reached into his shirt pocket, unwrapped a piece of gum, and handed it over.

As the boy chewed and chewed, she regretted she'd promised him some. Discreetly, she brushed her fingers over her mouth. That kiss had been hard to let go of. But Trey. There was always Trey, and that's how it should be. He hadn't flown before, and it had been a long time for her. Gum might help him.

Gage looked at his watch that had cost more than her mother's house, she was sure. "We'll be there in less than four hours."

Trey remained buckled into his seat, gazing out the window, so Bree concentrated on adult conversation. "How are you doing with everything?"

"Fine, thanks to all your prepping. The idea's become more acceptable to me in the past few days." She'd arranged phone calls for him to speak to his half brothers, Clint and Cameron. They wouldn't be total strangers when they met up at the restaurant in Franklin, where they lived with their families.

"You're an amazing man, you know that? It's been a lot to take in lately." She'd listened as Gage poured out his concerns, as well as some excitement at this new limb of his family tree.

"It's been more struggle than I'm used to, darling. But I can see my faith growing stronger through the challenges, due to the hardships, even."

"That's what we're told in the Bible will happen. I'm not sure I've believed it as I should. Certainly not when I'm going through something." Since that first silent prayer over the festival, they'd shared their faith more.

She pulled out her purse and wondered if it would be awkward to check her hair and makeup with him across from her. This meeting to see his twin half brothers was important to her too.

"Mommy, will we see bears?"

"I don't know, sweetie. Maybe? I don't want to see any up close though."

"I dooooo!"

The plane lifted into the air in the smoothest way possible. Bree sank back into the plush seat that was better than any commercial plane she'd flown in, which had not been many. She could get used to this.

Gage had eased back into his seat. "I brought bear spray. Taking a side jaunt to Gatlinburg was a stroke of genius, darling."

"I love how you call 'em like you see 'em." Smiling, Bree whipped her hand mirror out of her purse and arranged her hair. He'd seen every level of disheveled with her lately anyway, but still. "I appreciate your helping me balance the museum's books. So glad it was happy news." She freshened her lip gloss, then put her mirror away.

"You put on a great festival. Everybody said so, and they must've voted with their wallets, darling."

The two of them had worked through so many things, they'd developed an understanding of what made one another tick, it seemed. Whatever had happened to put them content with one another, she'd been walking on air the past few days. Either she and Gage had finally grown up or God had helped them to evolve. Probably both.

The plane landed, and once again, Bree saw the advantages of a private jet. In no time, they had deplaned and were in a black, sleek car headed toward the restaurant.

When they arrived, Gage reached for Trey's hand and then covered Bree's with his other hand. They both held on tighter than normal. "I'm glad you're here."

It was a simple, welcome message. "I feel the same way."

The Weavers had chosen a barbecue place near their homes. Once inside the mid-level restaurant with plastic black-and-white checked tablecloths, they didn't have the chance to speak with the hostess.

A man who could have been Gage's clone approached them and offered his hand. "You must be Gage. I'm Clint Weaver. Welcome to Tennessee, brother."

Gage introduced Bree and Trey, and then they walked back to where Cameron sat at a table. There was a family resemblance, but it wasn't quite as strong. The waiter brought crayons and an activity booklet for Trey, which kept him busy, to Bree's relief. For the next hour, she munched on some of the best barbecue she'd ever eaten and let the conversation envelop her as the men became acquainted.

It was thirty minutes more of lively conversation punctuated with oohs and aahs over moon pies, and then the visit ended. Bree had been happy to hang back from the conversation. She wasn't sure what, if anything, had been decided of the big topics. But before they parted, another meeting had been penciled in.

# Chapter 23

Gage turned the air conditioning up in the rental car, his mind abuzz with meeting his brothers for the first time. He and Bree and Trey had put a couple of hours' driving in since they'd left the barbecue place.

Bree sat in the front seat, and she leaned over, grabbed a light jacket and spread it across herself. "You've turned that thing up and down so many times you're gonna break it."

"I'm hot. Tennessee is far enough south to make the temps this time of year nearly like summer."

She tucked the jacket up a little closer around her neck and adjusted the car vents away from her. "Well, I'm freezing. Can't believe we're engaged in an age-old battle of the sexes, fussing over the thermostat settings."

"There you go again, making everything about history, darling," Gage teased.

"What makes you so sure what happened in the past doesn't relate to today?"

He tweaked the air conditioner, making it a bit warmer. This car had a sensitive touch, and it was getting a tad cold in there. She touched her fingers to her mouth and stifled a pretend laugh when she saw what he'd done.

"Look, darling, I call a truce on the history debate—and the temperature battles. I just spent more than an hour and enjoyed every minute with my new brothers—I won't call them half brothers—all thanks to you and your little museum that saved an old photo."

"There are legit reasons to preserve the past, Gage."

"You've made me a believer." He flipped his signal on and turned where the car navigation system indicated. "You deserve praise, and I'm afraid I haven't always made it easy. I really can't thank you enough for pursuing the photo."

"Well, I confess our time together has me looking at the future in a positive light. That includes both professionally and personally. Maybe I did cling to my passion for history a bit to the extreme."

He stopped at a light, leaned over, and kissed her. "For once, I'm grateful for a long traffic light." He kissed her again. "I think I'm becoming a big fan of compromise. And an even bigger fan of yours, darling."

"Mommy, can we play a game?" Trey piped up from his

booster seat where he'd been dozing in the back.

"Great idea. Which one? There's Hangman, or Would you Rather…."

Trey put his finger up to his cheek. "I spy with my little eye. That one."

For the next several miles, they called out something along the road that was a certain color and gave hints for the others to find it. When they tired of that game, Trey used his earbuds while he played some travel games that all fit in a metal box she'd brought along for him.

Bree touched Gage's arm resting on the center console, and he interlaced his fingers with hers, interested in everything she had to say. "I've been wanting to talk to you about parenting styles."

Well, maybe not everything. "We've got another hour or so until we get there. It's nice to have some downtime. You can let me know how to improve."

He stopped at a traffic light on red and she caught his eye. "You've been great. I'm the one that's been inflexible. When you first got to know Trey, I was too heavy-handed in my judging your parenting. I'm really sorry."

He didn't like to see any sadness in her eyes like he saw now. The light changed, and Gage pulled the car forward. "You're being too hard on yourself."

Bree pinned him with her gaze. "We both have differing styles—in just about everything. We can't gloss over that, but we can make it work to our advantage."

"Okay, well, once you gave me a time-out for giving Trey a

lollipop before dinner."

She laughed, and Gage couldn't help joining in.

More giggles came from the back seat. "Mommy didn't put you in time out, Daddy. No way Jose." Trey laughed and Gage savored the sound, feeling grateful for this child in his life.

He glanced at Bree. "Does it break some kind of rule that Galloway guys entertain ourselves and laugh at our own jokes sometimes?"

"Do whatever you want. It's fine by me. But if laughing at your own jokes is wrong, I don't wanna be right," she deadpanned.

Gage leaned back and grinned. "You know, this was a great idea to drive instead of fly. Look at those gorgeous mountains, everybody! The trees growing up the sides are a beautiful mix. The tops of the peaks look extra pretty, and they bump clear up to the sky." He caught the others looking at him. "Oops. For a second there, I became my dad and was back in my family's station wagon full of kids."

Trey called from the back, "Daddy, what's a station wagon?"

"Well, ours had extra-nice fancy wood panels on it, and there was room for a bunch of kids in the back. I think we borrowed it from my grandparents for our one cross-country road trip as a family."

"I love road trips," Trey said.

By the time they were within fifteen minutes of town, Trey had dozed off again. "What do you think?" Gage asked Bree softly. "I was hoping we could grab a bite and then check into the cabin. Or should we take Trey there and let him sleep more?"

"Nope. He's had the perfect nap. Besides, I was hoping we could walk along and see the shop fronts first. I'm always inspired by how they display their items. In a way, Murphy Museum is a retail store."

Gage checked his watch. Things were about on schedule for his plans for the evening. "It's too bad we can't stay here longer, but Trey's got school, and you and I have work to get back to."

Bree made a sad face. "Let's not think about that."

"I thought you loved working at the museum."

"I do. But I love spending time with you two more."

He found a place to park in the crowded area, pulled in, and shut off the car. Its windows were tinted dark so people couldn't see in, and Trey hadn't woken up. Gage leaned over and kissed Bree. Then he pulled back and studied her stunning blue eyes, prettier than any mountain range. "You know what, Bree Murphy? You made a great best friend. And you're making an even better ex-best friend."

She'd been giving him a dreamy look, until that last part. "Wait, you're booting me out as your best friend?"

"Think of it as an upgrade."

"Mommy?"

"Yeah. What is it, baby?"

"Can we get out and walk around? There's a big fuzzy bear."

"Sure, we can all go together."

He spotted the bigger-than-life decorative bear holding a sign with a restaurant menu. Gage planted a smooch on Bree's lips, and when he pulled away and prepared to exit the car, she let out a slight moan. "Do I need my sunglasses, do you think, darling?"

He put on the high-end designer aviator sunglasses he'd bought for the occasion. Bree grinned. "Sure, if it gets dark too quickly, just promise you'll let me lead you around." Bree snickered.

"Or I could just put them in my pocket. Be honest, do these make me look like Leo?"

She squinted. "You mean your brother the artist?"

"No, Leo the iconic actor."

"Well, sure. You could be twins. The glasses are the same anyway."

He flipped the visor. Maybe she was teasing him, but he still liked the look.

"Okay, buddy," Gage called over the seat. "Thanks for waiting for me to come around and get you. When we're in crowds like this, we need to all watch out for each other."

"Okay, Daddy. I'll be careful."

They managed to leave the car, only after Bree considered aloud whether to take her purse or to tuck it under the seat and let Gage pay for everything. She opted to have her own things with her.

"We've done planes and automobiles today. Trains are all that's left," she said, grabbing onto his elbow. He covered her hand with his, and when Trey grabbed her other hand, a warm, satisfied feeling came over Gage. Maybe God had planned a family for him after all.

They started down the crowded street. "Toys!" Trey darted into a little store with Bree on his heals. Gage stayed out on the sidewalk and inhaled the food scents coming from a few nearby restaurants. Chocolate wafted up from a fudge shop. Trey sailed back out with a little toy bear, and Gage slowed him down. He didn't want him to trip over the sidewalks made of gigantic chunks of dark-gray stone that went up and over hills. Gage enjoyed holding Bree's hand and reviewed his day as he took in the ambiance of the clear evening sky and strings of twinkle lights that were tied among the little shops.

Lunch with his brothers had been one highlight. A skilled carpenter, Clint worked on some of the most prestigious homes in the Midwest and showed Gage photos. Cameron's talents were in the photography field, which had been just what Gage needed to spark an idea for later.

"Cookies!" Trey trotted toward little metal chairs and tables sitting out in front of the shop with a light-up sign promoting cookies.

Bree leaned toward him with raised eyebrows "Oh, we have a history with cookies. Remember what kind they served when we met in second grade?"

Gage squeezed her hand. If he was going to leave this sky behind for precious minutes to wait in the winding line in the store, it would be for cookies. "How could I forget? Snickerdoodles."

By the time each one had scarfed down two snickerdoodles, Gage had described to Trey how he'd met his mom in school. They were all covered in cinnamon, so Bree went back and grabbed a handful of napkins.

When they started walking again, the sidewalks seemed to be even more crowded with visitors. "Will we be eating dinner here? I'm partial to steak," Gage said.

"I can't hold any more right now," Bree said, grinning from ear to ear. "Those were two monstrous cookies." She laughed as if she wasn't bothered at all by baked goods as big as their heads.

"Well, I'll call ahead, and we can have night-time snacks on the way back on our plane." They walked past a big sign and Gage pointed to it. "Who wants to ride the tramway up the mountain?"

Trey's hand shot into the air, and he jumped up and down. "Me. Me. Me."

A few minutes later, they were in the glass box with windows all around, swinging from an aerial wire.

Gage put his arm around Bree's shoulders as they hung onto the overhead straps and Trey sat in a seat. "You seem a little pale. Everything okay?"

She only looked at him, instead of out the windows like the other tourists did. "Not crazy about heights. But I'll be okay."

He moved closer. "Why didn't you say something? We didn't have to do this."

"Because I thought you two would enjoy it, and I'm okay. I don't want to pass on my issues to him."

"I like how you think about Trey and the impact things have on him. You're really great."

She gave him a smile through pale lips. "I can't wait to get off this mountain."

"It won't be long until we jet back to Fair Creek."

She nodded and her expression was unreadable.

The tram reached the top, and they stayed on. Then it slowly made its way down to the bottom, and he treasured the time holding Bree more than he did watching the scenery.

In too short a time, they were in his plane heading back.

Gage leaned forward in his seat and took a bite of tortilla chips loaded with cheese, while he enjoyed Bree chowing down on pita bread slathered in humus. "You can see why I'm never bothered by skipping a restaurant meal."

"Your crew is really something." She glanced at Trey, who ate Cracker Jacks and some grapes while he watched a movie. "Being with you is such a treat. Sometimes, when I only had sippy cups and goldfish crackers with Trey, I wondered if I'd get into the adult zone again."

He reached over and tucked a strand of her hair behind her ears. "I'd say you've arrived. There's nothing like having all the advantages of grown-ups."

"You're so right. I feel lucky to have both worlds."

For once, he understood what people saw in having a wife and kids. Before he knew it, he'd be leaving them in Fair Creek. He wasn't looking forward to it. But what choice did he have?

# Chapter 24

Bree stood at the counter in the Murphy Museum and folded another T-shirt before dropping it into the storage box. She stared out the front window at an overcast sky that showed various shades of gray, just like her mood.

Gage had brought them home on his jet a couple of weeks ago--ten days and 12 hours, to be exact. Since their Tennessee trip, she'd had trouble keeping thoughts of Gage in the friend zone. He called every day, and yesterday he'd called twice.

His deep voice asking for Trey did her in every time. He was nice to her, and they chatted sometimes. But it was hard to know how he felt through a phone line.

*Don't ruin a beautiful friendship.* She might as well write that mantra on her forehead, for all the good it did.

From the corner of her eye, she detected Trey coming down the stairs in his socks with Jo close on his heels, until he trudged into the room. He flopped across the upholstered seat of a chair for visitors. They often fell down the rabbit hole like Alice in Wonderland when hunting for information about their family trees and needed to sit.

"What're you doing, honey? Your show's not over yet, is it?"

Jo straightened some brochures on top of a case of memorabilia, then spread out her hands with both palms turned up. "He's restless so I said we'd come and bug you."

Bree straightened her shoulders, for Trey as much as for herself. Leaving the shirts, she forced a bounce into her step as she walked over and stood by Trey.

"Want to play games? We've got a closetful."

"There's nothin' to do." Maybe spending time on the farm hadn't been such a good idea, since the museum and home had lost its appeal.

Jo studied the boy, looked at Bree, and quirked an eyebrow. "He's short on fuel. Not sure you're doing much better."

Bree shrugged. "It's the after-festival slump. I invited you to perk us up."

"There's not a lot I can do. Maybe you're both missing a certain someone."

Bree focused on the lone bud in a vase that needed dumped in the trash, and she went and did that. They'd been just fine before Gage came into their lives. Having him here permanently was never in the picture.

When she returned, she put her hands on her hips. "We're fine on our own. Right, Trey?"

Trey sat up and glanced at Jo, where his brown eyes remained on her as she answered. "Well, if I had someone who looked at me the way Gage looks at you, I'd get a new philosophy."

Someone knocked on the door. She'd just closed the museum for the day, and no one ever visited after hours. She looked in the peephole. Gage? She blinked and looked again.

With effort, she fought the urge to yank the door open and throw herself into the man's arms. *Play it cool, Bree.* She stood back and opened the door like he was the pizza man making a delivery.

She wouldn't jeopardize a great friendship for a sketchy chance at a relationship.

Outside on the porch, Gage pinned her with his gaze, and she was pretty sure that he could see right through her. "There for a minute, I thought you weren't home, darling."

She beamed at him in a carefree way, she hoped. "Oh, come on in. I was just having a fascinating conversation with our son. But I thought you weren't coming until tomorrow."

"I couldn't wait any longer to see you." Butterflies danced in her stomach, except she knew he meant Trey.

Didn't he?

"Daddy!" Trey ran to them and jumped up and down. "I missed you, Daddy!"

Gage couldn't believe the tight grip of Trey's arms wrapped around his legs in a bear hug. Although he was trying to rein in his heartbeat after seeing Bree again, Trey's gesture warmed his heart.

He bent down to the boy's level. "I missed you, buddy. You've grown like a weed since last time I saw you." He tickled Trey's stomach and the boy giggled.

Bringing Trey along in his arms as he went, Gage stood. Bree's dazzling smile and the blue of her eyes brought him right back to wanting to be with her, to never leave her.

"Your Mommy's as pretty as ever." He spoke over Trey's head.

Woah. He'd given himself a talking-to about keeping it casual. They hadn't made any commitments to one another, except where Trey was concerned.

"Well, it's nice to see you, Gage." Jo's voice carried over from across the room. The woman must have seen they were both tongue-tied. "Trey, why don't we go upstairs and let your parents have a chat?"

"Oh, I almost forgot. I've got a surprise for Trey."

"For me?" The little boy's eyes widened, and Gage gestured for Bree to lead the way as he carried Trey outside.

Covering the short distance to the pickup truck in long strides, urgent barks came from inside the cab. Since it wasn't hot out, he'd left the windows cracked.

"A puppy!" Trey shrieked and started wriggling to get down.

"His name's Duke." The museum was on a quiet street and when Trey's feet reached the ground, Gage let the dog out.

The pup jumped and ran around.

Trey hopped up on a little picnic table out on the lawn. When the dog reached him on the bench seat, Trey climbed up on the tabletop. Duke's training must have flown from the dog's mind, judging from his nonstop jumping and barking.

"Duke! Duke!" The boy screamed and laughed and seemed to have the best time.

Gage didn't dare look at Bree, until the boy and dog were clearly enjoying each other, with Trey still on the table and safe.

Finally, he couldn't avoid her any longer and glanced Bree's way. He'd seen that look before, when he'd gone rogue and gotten a different golf cart. "He's very cute." Her words were clipped.

"Well, I think Trey's been missing me." He swallowed, aware of how much he wanted her to feel the same. "I know I've wanted to see him a lot more."

She touched his arm for a moment. "We've both missed you. We're all connected, Gage, more than I'd have thought possible in such a short time." The corners of her mouth twitched up. "At least, I was until you brought an unruly animal here--that my child's falling in love with."

"I thought you wanted a farm boy. He's *our* child." Gage reached up and tucked her hair behind her ear. "Falling in love is out of a person's control, darling."

She leaned closer and their eyes locked. "So I've been told."

When he bridged the gap, their kiss seemed natural and ended way too soon.

He needed to stay on track here. "Every kid needs a dog. Duke's excited right now, but my brothers have been training him. He'll settle in. You'll see. And you can leave him at the farm as much as you want."

"I don't think you know much about kids. Trey's not going to want to part with him, Gage."

"I may have a lot to learn about kids, but I know what it's like not wanting to part with something, or someone."

He touched her cheek that was soft and warm, then tore his gaze from hers, went toward the picnic table and reached for Trey's hand. "I'm so glad you met Duke. You're a brave boy. Now it's time to say goodbye."

He picked up Trey and felt him trembling. "But he's mine," he said. The child didn't make any attempt to get close to the dog, though.

Had he made a mistake? Gage wished for reassurance, which he hadn't found as a parent, and he'd never needed before in any area of his life.

Bree came up beside him and slipped Trey from his arms. "Daddy's given Duke to you and he's going to help you with him. Now it's yours and Duke's bedtime, so let's say good night."

With soothing words and by holding the dog close, Gage calmed Duke so that the child could pat his head. "What kind of dog is he, Daddy?"

"He's a German Shepherd. I got him because he's a good

protector for you and Mommy."

Trey's eyelids drooped. But the sparkle was just as bright, as Bree handed him off to Jo, who started to carry him inside. "I love Duke." It came out more like "wuv," he was so sleepy.

They were finally alone, if he didn't count Duke. "Do you think you'll ever be able to forgive me for the dog?"

She held Duke's paw where it rested on Gage's arm. "We have a lifetime for you to try, and that's good enough for me."

He laughed, and it had been too long since he had. "Sometimes I'm afraid my approach to life is rubbing off on you." Duke let out a low, puppy howl and Bree rubbed his tummy to distract him. "Hate to say it, darling. This dog needs to go to bed, and I flew long and hard to be here, only to turn right back around."

"What're we going to do, Gage?"

He brushed his lips across hers, and the dog squirmed. "I told you my brothers will help with Duke in every way."

"I meant about us, you and me?"

Duke had fallen asleep and was cradled in his arms. "Do I look like a man who has all the answers? I'm just going on that thing they say."

"Which thing?"

His charge stirred and Gage pivoted toward the truck and headed off. "Remind me to tell you sometime."

# Chapter 25

Bree couldn't believe Gage had left only a week ago.

She tossed the paper onto the counter, happy the school hadn't gone to digital reports like all the others. Trey's latest teacher's report said he was struggling to pay attention. She hadn't gotten on him too much about it, since she could relate and worried his listless attitude came from her.

"So, what's your next big project?" Kristin had stopped over when she'd told her she had the blahs.

"Nothing is in the works at this point."

Kristin put Dale Murphy's special cowboy boots away for the season and gave Bree her brightest smile. "Well, this isn't unusual. You know there's always a letdown after the festival. All that build-up, and then it's over."

Bree fiddled with a notepad of Dale and decided to keep it for herself. "True. This just feels different. Jo stayed on for a few days to help out, but there's nothing anyone can do."

"To state the obvious, could you be missing Gage?"

She nodded. "Yes, but we've got our separate lives. And with the distance, I'm afraid we'll end up just friends again. Or worse, I might lose Gage as a friend, too."

"Bree! I think you'd better look out front." Jo stood at the top of the stairs, waving her hands like she was excited about something.

Must be nice.

"Why? I'm well aware of the weather. The forecast is gray and more gray."

Jo clapped her hands. "I mean it, Breezy. You're going to want to see what's going on outside."

Bree hurried thru the foyer and opened the front door with more energy than she thought she had in her. She gasped, let out a squeal, and ran out the door.

An ornate, old-fashioned carriage had been parked on the museum's front lawn. A bundle of balloons floated up from its roof. She was halfway there when Gage stepped out, his lean frame accentuated by a classic western shirt, jeans that hugged his muscular thighs, and a wide-brimmed cowboy hat.

He looked so scrumptious that Bree squealed again. She couldn't help herself.

Then she was beside him and he kissed her. "Bree, I've missed you, darling."

Trey climbed out of the carriage dressed as a miniature Gage.

"Daddy said he missed us a whole lot, Mommy. We ate cookies on the way. Duke's having his cookie in the carriage 'cause he'd tear things up if he came out."

Bree's heart was so full she thought it would burst. She stood close to her two favorite men and beamed. "You're supposed to be in DC. Where'd you get this gorgeous carriage and this handsome boy?"

Gage reached down and patted Trey's head. "God gave us this wonderful boy. And I don't want to spend any more time away from you two. The carriage is for showing me the goodness in history."

Bree's heart rate kicked up. Could he really mean it, after he thrived on adventure? "What about your work?"

"I'm at the point where I value a family and tradition and rootedness more than anything. You, Trey, and my family, can make a bonfire on the farm exciting." He grinned, and she felt his sincerity all the way down to her toes. "I wanted to do something special for you. Wyatt's buddy had this vintage carriage. Figured you'd research its history. All I want is to ride in it with you."

She wouldn't cry, she told herself. But tears pricked behind her eyes, and she saw Gage through a haze. "It's perfcet. I love it. I thought I could live without you but I'm not doing a very good job of it—and it hasn't even been a week. I need you, Gage."

"That's the thing people say, 'Find someone you can't live without.' You're that someone for me. I've been working it out so I can permanently be on the farm."

"Are you sure that'll make you happy?"

"I'm happy wherever you are, darling, if you'll have me."

Trey looked up at Gage with such adoration in his eyes that Bree had to swallow the lump in her throat.

Gage dropped down on one knee in front of her with a box in his palm. Her hands flew to her mouth, and her breath caught in her throat.

"Bree Skye Murphy, would you do me the honor of becoming my wife? I love you and want to be with you."

"Yes! I'll marry you. I'm so grateful God brought you into my life again."

He stood and slipped a ring on her finger. "This was my mother's."

She exhaled in surprise. "I'll treasure it always." His kiss tasted of cinnamon and was so tender she never wanted it to end.

"Daddy, can we go for a ride?"

"We're going to, Trey. Do you want to change your name to Galloway?"

Their son beamed and put his little fist in the air. "Yay, I'm gonna be a Galloway!"

"You always were, son."

Bree had never heard sweeter words.

"Oh, and there's one more thing. Come on out, guys."

Clint and Cameron, Gage's new-found brothers, stepped out from behind the carriage, with Duke. Gage took the dog in his arms.

"We wouldn't want to miss this for the world, and we missed so much of the Galloways already. Say cheese, Bree," Cameron said. He held up an old camera and snapped photos.

Clint spoke quietly. "You brought us together, and we're so grateful. We could see Gage was smitten with you, so we offered to come and capture his proposal on film."

"I'd love to get some family photos. You three stand over there with Duke."

Bree welcomed a chance to stand close again. The camera clicked and she knew these were photos she'd always cherish.

"Now, stand next to your mommy, and Gage, would you plant a kiss on Bree?"

"I'd be more than happy to."

His lips were warm and the kiss was full of promise.

Gage reluctantly pulled away, still holding her close. "Are you ready for a chariot ride?"

Bree nodded.

"I'm your driver," Clint said.

With Gage holding her hand, Bree climbed into the carriage, and he joined her. Trey hopped up and sat in between them and Gage put Duke in the boy's lap. Bree, Gage, Trey, and Duke rode down Main Street while the camera captured every historic moment.

Would you like to read more about the Galloway Sons of Fair Creek? *Her Billionaire Cowboy's Secret Heir: A Galloway Sons Farm Novel* (Christmas in Fair Creek, Book 4)  is Miles Galloway's story and it's the next book in the series.

Books in the Galloway Sons Farm Series

*Her Billionaire Cowboy's Twin Heirs:*
*Christmas in Fair Creek (A Fair Creek Romance, prequel)*

*Her Billionaire Cowboy's Second Chance:*
*Galloway Sons Farm (A Fair Creek Romance, Book 1)*

*Her Billionaire Cowboy's Triplets:*
*Galloway Sons Farm (Christmas in Fair Creek, Book 2)*

*Her Billionaire Cowboy's Best Friend:*
*Galloway Sons Farm (A Fair Creek Romance, Book 3)*

*Her Billionaire Cowboy's Secret Heir:*
*A Galloway Sons Farm Novel (Christmas in Fair Creek, Book 4)*

*Her Billionaire Cowboy's Pretend Proposal:*
*Galloway Sons Farm (A Fair Creek Romance, Book 5)*

*Her Billionaire Cowboy's Last Chance:*
*Galloway Sons Farm (A Fair Creek Romance, Book 6)*

*Her Billionaire Cowboy's Christmas Wish:*
*Galloway Sons Farm (Christmas in Fair Creek, Book 7)*

# About the Author

Cathy Shouse writes inspirational cowboy romance. Her Fair Creek series, set in Indiana, features the Galloway brothers of Galloway Sons Farm. Much like the characters in her stories, Cathy once lived on a farm in "small town" Indiana where she first fell in love with cowboys while visiting the rodeo every summer.

She loves to stay in touch with readers. Sign up to receive her newsletter at: www.cathyshouse.com where you'll get free books, exclusive bonus content, and news of her releases and sales.

If you liked this book, please take a moment to review it! Authors (including Cathy) really appreciate this, and it helps draw more readers to books they might like. Thanks!

www.ingramcontent.com/pod-product-compliance
Lightning Source LLC
Chambersburg PA
CBHW061436210726
48287CB00007B/2238